"Thank you," he said, which somehow seemed to be just for her being there, for letting him breathe in her essence.

Ronnie licked her lips, but managed to stop herself from brushing back her hair with her gloved hand. "Don't do that," she said.

"Do what?"

"Look at me like that."

"Like what?"

Ronnie blushed so hard she could feel it prickle her scalp. "Like you think you've got some kind of chance with me. Like maybe the fact that we both grew up here somehow entitles you to a shot. I'm not some kind of wild deer or rabbit you can hunt down or snare *or* seduce."

The corner of his mouth quirked up. "Your mother said you weren't engaged to Louis yet."

ALSO BY TERRI DARLING

Downhill Rush

What a Man Wants

Second Chances

Last One to Hide

COLLECTIONS

Love Sneaks In

Love Sneaks In Again

Love Snuck

Love Steps Up

Love Steps Up Again

Love Steps Up Deluxe

TERRI DARLING

Cinnamon Hearts

fiero
PUBLISHING

Published in electronic form 2013 by Fiero Publishing
Published in trade paper 2013 by Fiero Publsihing
www.fieropublishing.com
Book and cover design copyright © 2013 by Fiero Publishing
Cover design by Terry Hayman/Fiero Publishing
Cover art copyright © omgimages/123RF Stock Photo and karenr/123RF Stock Photo

ISBN-13: 978-1927920060

ISBN-10: 192792006X

First Print Edition: December 2013

For Hazel and Bute, who made
"small town" something special.

Cinnamon Hearts

1

DECEMBER 23, but Ronnie was ready to leave the second she walked in the door. It was like stepping into a human-sized meat grinder where the spinning blades were relatives, their arms and kisses and cries all slashing and cutting up her snowy coat and hat to a background of the Andrews Sisters' *Jingle Bells* and the smell of a roast ham and shortbread cookies and eggnog and cinnamon.

Love the unlovable woman! Make her feel loved! Home! Happy!

And she'll just fake that it's working, okay? Okay!

"—and when Louis arrives—he didn't come with you?" Her apple dumpling mother paused her welcome gush for just a second, shushing her six-year-old grandson Nick to one side so she could check the entryway and sidewalk behind Ronnie's shoulder before plunging on.

Ronnie tugged off her hat and shook out her hair. "Negatory," she drawled.

"I wanted him to meet the Stephanopoluses," her mother continued on like she hadn't heard. "You remember

Andreas Stephanopolus? He's here tonight with his wife, and he's promised to take us on a tour of the Putter's Ridge development tomorrow afternoon. You know, the one with the view over the valley? Perfect for young families, all wired up for telecommuting."

And there it was. The other reason this had to be a short trip. Why every trip here these last few years kept getting shorter and shorter. Her mother, her whole family really, never really looked at *her*. They only saw what they wanted to see.

"Mom? Um…"

"Everyone thought it would be dead with the slow recovery and all—"

"If you'd just…"

"—but people had already bought six of the properties, sunk their life savings into them, and Andreas's third *son* convinced his father that…"

"Evelyn! Give our eldest some room to breathe!"

It was Ronnie's father at last, her one refuge. His leonine head of hair, once as fiery red as Ronnie's but now a distinguished silver, swung out of the kitchen a few dignified steps behind the greeting mob of Ronnie's mother, whirlwind little nephew Nick, round-cheeked sister Emma, rangy brother Alexander, and Alex's wife Suzie.

Together, the group filled the front entrance so completely that Ronnie couldn't have pushed through if she'd wanted to, making the prospect of just turning around and running almost irresistible.

Except that the taxi which had brought her from the train station had already left and there was blizzard warning for the evening. Bad thing to be running through while rolling a monster suitcase behind you and crying your eyes out.

Then somehow her father had actually managed to slip his rangy frame through the greeters and even nudge his well-cushioned wife to one side, so that he could put a hand on either side of Ronnie's shoulders and face her square on. Her father's considering look from underneath his untrimmed, bushy eyebrows was the last straw for Ronnie and she felt herself shaking apart from the inside out. A few seconds and she was going to fall into pieces like one of those cheap plastic doll houses she and Emma always used to scream in joy over on Christmas morning and destroy by the second or third day of hard play.

Well, Ronnie had been destroyed in just that way, hadn't she. Played with, broken, and found wanting. Unlovable.

"Knucklehead isn't coming, is he?" her father said quietly under the background music from the living room. The remnants of his Irish lilt made it even softer.

Ronnie shook her head, fighting hard to hold it together as her mother sucked in a sharp breath.

"Good," her father said.

"What?" said Ronnie's mother.

"Really?" Ronnie added, looking at him in the doubting way she fell into around him. Because she could. Because he was the one man she truly never doubted.

"*Why?*" said Ronnie's mother.

And before Ronnie could deliver her carefully-prepared statement about how she and Louis just wanted different things in life (yeah, like she wanted him and he didn't want her), her father swung his large face towards her mother and said, "Because he never liked the right candy."

"Colin Cleary!" cried Ronnie's mother.

"It's true!" Ronnie's dad pouted at her. "He was always going for the caramel chocolate fancies you put out."

"Everyone loves those," Ronnie's mother said. "Every Christmas…"

"I know. I know. But cinnamon heart candies…"

"Only you and Ronnie eat those."

"Because *she* has taste."

"And everyone else, the rest of the Cleary family, the whole rest of the world, doesn't?"

"Apparently not."

"Let me guess—it's an Irish thing."

"Now that you mention it…"

Ronnie's head was whipping so fast back and forth between her parents' traditional ping-pong exchange that she actually found herself smiling, which both of her parents caught at the same time, stopped, and turned back to her.

"Welcome home, my darling," her mother said, and her father wrapped her up in the kind of bear hug only he had ever had the audacity to give her.

When she emerged from his Old Spice embrace, she was

still smiling, eyes wet, but actually smiling. When everyone wasn't focused on *her*, specifically, there were a few things to like about being home. "Thanks Mom and Dad. And Nick, Emma, Alex, Suzie. Am I the last one in?"

"Everyone but Santa Claus!" said Nick, again underfoot. He also had the Cleary red hair, even though it had skipped his father, Alex, who had his mother's chestnut hair and solid build.

"Uncle Sean and Margery are here for dinner," Emma said. Margery and Ronnie's father's brother had been living together for almost as long as Ronnie could remember, but tradition, or some kind of Irish stubbornness, kept the Cleary's from calling her *Aunt* Margery. "And I brought along Jeff. You remember him from those pictures I sent."

"I do."

"And Louis is *not* coming for sure?" said her mother.

It cut a painful chunk off Ronnie's smile, but she held onto the rest as she shook her head. "I do not have a boyfriend with me at this time, but I *do* have..."—she paused for dramatic effect and caught Nick with her gaze—"a very large suitcase which is about sixty-five percent filled with presents that I could really use some help putting around the tree."

"I can do that!" shouted Nick.

"Can you do it without pawing through my underwear?"

The six-year-old made a stinky face and nodded vigorously.

"Then have at 'er, Nick."

Her little nephew darted around her to grab the handle of the suitcase that weighed more than he did, screamed in protest when his father, Alex, stepped forward to help, and managed to pull it over onto himself just enough to roll it on its wheels. Then he inched his way, puffing and grinning like the suitcase was as heavy as a fridge and he was a professional mover, through the parting crowd and down the hall to the living room. Alex, bless his overprotective heart, inched along behind him, ready to leap to the rescue if his son was suddenly crushed by Aunt Ronnie's suitcase of doom.

"I also have," said Ronnie to the remaining door crowd of her parents, younger sister Emma, and Alex's Suzie, "something just for those of us who can appreciate them..."

She reached into the deep pockets of her coat and drew out, one from each, two paper-and-cellophane bags from the sweets shop where she worked in the city, happy to see they hadn't been crushed in the meat-grinder greeting.

She grinned as she held them high and saw her father's eyes go big in anticipation. Her grin increased when she shared the joke of their father's sweet tooth in a quick, nonverbal exchange with Emma. The two of them actually laughed when their mother grabbed their father's arm in a kind of horror, like their pop was a ravenous sugar beast who might drool and leap at any moment.

Might not be that far from the truth.

"Wait!" called an unfamiliar baritone from down the hall. "Are those from…Chester's?"

Ronnie had to lean sideways to see around her father and Suzie, but seeing the owner of the voice made nothing clearer. He was shorter than Ronnie's father, barely taller than Ronnie herself, actually, with a dark chocolate gaze, curly hair, and a very square, muscular build, made more obvious when he stood near the stretched-out wiriness of Ronnie's dad. Something about his demeanor, though, said port in a storm. A very calm strength. But she remembered that this macho power thing was what had originally attracted her to Louis too, and look how well that had turned out.

"Ronnie," her mother jumped in, "this is Andreas and Antonia's son, Marcario Stephanopolus." She turned to him. "Did I get that right?"

"Mark," he said, and grinned in such a self-assured male way that Ronnie's heart fluttered a little. Again like Louis. Like Ronnie couldn't get enough of arrogant males. A groupie to a rock star. A geek to a prince. She hadn't realized it was such a bad pattern for her. Or maybe it was just the weird juxtaposition of this guy's movie star looks against her memory of what he was like as a kid. Because she remembered his name. And though the muscles and hair and even the adult face shape were different, the easy smile she'd gone so silly over back then was still the same.

"Hi," Ronnie said. "We took swimming classes together one time, right?"

He nodded. "Back in...what? Grade three?"

"You in three. I was two years behind you. You were always swimming faster than everyone to show off."

"Sounds like me. But you were good at something..."

Ronnie felt her face color and tried to cover it with a smirk. "Floating. I was always good at floating."

"While I sank like a stone. I remember that now. Had to skull like mad to stay up."

"And now you're..."

"Back at school. Doing an MBA."

"At Harvard!" piped in Ronnie's mother.

"Planning on helping my dad's construction business evolve. Keep it in the family."

"Which is soooo nice," Ronnie's mother said meaningfully to Ronnie, presumably reminded of her long-held dream Ronnie would go back to school, finish her web designer degree and then return to Mayville and somehow help out at her father's law practice, since Emma was getting her teaching degree a couple states away and Alexander had joined the US Army, of all things.

"And you're in business too, I understand," Mark said to Ronnie now.

"I dropped *out* of web design," she said. "I make candies."

"I know that."

Then he stared intently at her, apparently oblivious to how Suzie and Emma kept shooting their gazes between her and Mark. It made Ronnie want to jump on both of them like she used to when they were bratty little playmates always in cahoots against big sister Ronnie. Didn't they get that Ronnie was in mourning? Sure, she'd told them all she was never going to marry, never going to settle down, despite how she and

Louis practically lived together, but jumping directly from one boyfriend to another was a little much even for someone as prickly and tradition-flouting as her. Besides, if she ever did manage to move on, it would never be with someone here, in the town she grew up in. She'd worked too hard to get out of here. And while she still might not have found out where she belonged, she'd found *parts* of it. With Louis, she'd thought she'd found *all* of it...

Mark Stephanopolus was still staring at her.

"*What?*" she demanded.

"Chester's Sweets," he said slowly and tapped his head like he'd missed something obvious. "Your sister told me earlier that you worked at a candy factory. She didn't say it was the premiere candy store in Chicago. I drop in there whenever I fly into Chicago."

"I'm... Uh. Emma?" Ronnie looked at her hands and realized she was still holding up two bags of Chester's Christmas peanut brittle, something that really *was* her. She and Rolf, the co-owner and head chocolatier at Chester's had dreamed this up back in mid-October, experimented with it for four weekends running to get the right mix of nutmeg and orange worked into the mix. Now it was flying off their shelves. A bona fide hit. It had meant a lovely bonus for her this year *and* an unexpected demand that she take the couple of days leading up to Christmas and the whole week after Christmas off, despite it being a peak sales time. Rolf and Chester had apparently known her relationship with Louis was set to implode at least two weeks before it actually had, and they'd made provisions for some seasonal help to cover for her absence.

"Because broken hearts and sweets don't mix, dearest," Chester had said, with Rolf smiling sympathetically at his shoulder. "You go and bathe in the love of your family."

"You mean choke on it?"

"Smunchkin, they might be difficult and small town, but I've heard you talk about them enough to know that they love you lots. And *that* is what you need right now. Lots and lots and lots of love. You bathe in it. Make sure it fills you up to here." He'd patted the underside of Rolf's fleshy chin. "And only when you're right full of love do you come back here and put it into your creations."

Which meant he might as well have fired her, Ronnie thought now. Because even if she could blithely accept all her family's love and the unspoken expectations that flowed with it, it would still just pour in, then dribble out through the hole Louis had punched in her heart.

"You never work the counters there," Mark Stephanopolus said now, yanking her back to her parents' front entryway, where she stood still dumbly holding up two bags of hers and Rolf's creations. "I'd have remembered your face."

"No, I just...make candies," she mumbled. "Some marzipan. Some chocolates. Mostly candies."

"And Chester's Christmas Brittle." His eyes were now fixed on the bags she still held up. She could have sworn he was drooling as much as Ronnie's father. Of course. He didn't really even see Ronnie, just the candy. Which, in a way, was more honest than Louis, who'd drooled over her body and *pretended* he'd really been interested in her mind, heart, and soul.

She managed a smile. "Rolf and I came up with it."

"Rolf?"

"My co-confectioner, though his specialty is chocolates."

Mark stared at her for a moment like he was looking for something in her face, then turned with gusto to Ronnie's father and said in a confiding tone. "I know at least three guys I went to Northwestern with who have sworn they will kill anyone who sneaks any of their private stashes of Chester's Christmas Brittle. They mailed me some and I instantly understood why. Had to pick up more on my way home here for Christmas. Your daughter and Rolf, Sir, are demons who make things that foster selfish and ravenous behavior."

Ronnie's father nodded seriously at him, then turned abruptly towards Ronnie. "I need to try some of that brittle, my darling. Right now."

"Me too!" said Mark.

"Shhh!" said Ronnie's mother with a significant glance down the hall where Alex and Nick had only just vanished into the living room. Then she held out her hand, as did Suzie and Emma. "Us too."

Ronnie laughed and offered one bag to her mother, sister, and sister-in-law; one bag to her father and Mark.

The speed and munching satisfaction with which everything was devoured made her rethink all the presents she'd bought for her family. Maybe she should have just bought sweets.

As they ate, she finally shook out her long red hair and shrugged off her heavy wool coat and boots. When she stepped back from hanging it up in the front hall closet to the right of the front door, she was amused to see Mark, with his mouth full of brittle, freeze in place, staring at her with his eyes wide.

She gave a mini-snort and smoothed down the tight green sweater over the tops of her jeans. She knew the sweater brought out her eye color and complimented the fiery orange of her hair. Okay, so Harvard boy could be distracted by a good figure as well as good candy. Which made him at least a Cro-Magnon like Louis. How very nice for him.

But like her dad said, guys like Louis and this man, certainly all the male classmates she'd had in her computer courses at University of Chicago, wanted sweets and chocolates. And while Ronnie might be able to *produce* those things, what she really *was* was red hot cinnamon. Yes, that was much better than the shiny toy analogy. And better than calling herself a groupie or a geek. She was a cinnamon candy—sweet outside but too hot to predict inside. Or maybe just too hot to keep around. Get past her shell, like Louis had done, and you spat her out, moved on.

A moment later, all the brittle had been devoured. Ronnie's mother had already disappeared back to the kitchen where she said she'd left Margery with the final prep. Her father gave a last, longing look into both of the empty bags, sighed, and gestured for the rest of them to proceed to the living room. Ronnie found herself uncomfortably bumped up against Mark Stephanopolus as she padded along in her sock feet, then smirked when he elaborately stepped back and waved her ahead of him.

"What's that for?" she murmured as she passed. "Want to see the rear view? Or just done with talking to me?"

"Maybe both?" he murmured back.

She sniffed a little, then got annoyed at herself for the self-pity and determined then and there to drop it. Louis was gone. She had to just face it. She needed, like Chester and Rolf had said, to just enjoy her family, if possible, get her heart back together again, and move on.

It wasn't until she was three steps into the living room that she became aware of the hush.

She looked up to find everyone staring at her expectantly, including her uncle and the couple she almost recognized as Mr. and Mrs. Stephanopolus. A very full room. The music had been turned down to barely audible. She scanned all their face nervously, ending up on her father's face with a pleading look.

"The tree," he whispered.

"Ah. Right." She brushed back her hair behind her ears and tried to remember who she was supposed to be—the cheery eldest daughter returned home for Christmas Eve from the big city. She smiled, somewhat maniacally, she feared. "I mean…ooooh. Ahhhh. *That* is a Christmas tree."

Which it truly was. Her mother and father had gone all out this year, maybe because it was the first time the whole clan had been together in three years. Alex had probably even come home early with his family to help them buy it and bring it in.

Because the tree was an enormous fir tree, filling an entire end of the usually cavernous-feeling living room. She realized she could smell its sap and needles now. Actually, she'd probably smelled them from the moment she'd walked in but just lumped them all together in her head with the other scents that said Christmas.

But that woodsy, clean scent *really* said it, didn't it? The tree twinkled with deep blue LED lights and the bushy top few branches almost brushed the ten-foot ceilings, with the traditional Cleary Christmas angel in the center on top— all white dress, gold wings, a tiny electric candle held up in each hand. It irrationally threatened to make her carefully-sustained cheeriness, drop right out through her socks.

Because it represented hope to her. It had fed her little girl dreams of growing up to be more than a farmer or shopkeeper's wife, to get out and see the world, do big things. And yet where had that gotten her? She'd gone to Chicago, but dropped out of university to *cook* of all things, and ended up putting all her hopes for greatness into a man who'd gone and cheated on her, then told her she just wasn't good enough for him. Thanks, angel.

"Yes, *that* is a Christmas tree," her father said from where he'd stepped up to stand behind her. He wrapped an arm around her shoulders again like he sensed just how much she needed the extra support, and he gave her a little squeeze.

"And now that it's had its proper acknowledgement from the last of the Cleary clan to arrive," he went on, "I do believe it is time for a Christmas Eve feast for family and friends, followed by song, visiting, drinks both alcoholic and non,"— he gave a meaningful glance down at Nick, who was down on his bum by the tree, carefully reading the little hints Ronnie had scrawled on each of the gifts she'd wrapped—"then plans for the morrow, and rest for all, both the just and the unjust."

He conspicuously looked at the ceiling on "unjust" as he always did, careful not to single anyone out. Another long-running Cleary joke (an allusion to Portia's speech to Shylock in *The Merchant of Venice*, for Pete's sake) that Mark Stephanopolus, Ronnie noted in passing, seemed to enjoy thoroughly. Either the guy was really smart or a real suck-up. Or both, like Louis had been. Ronnie had once found that sort of charming; then she'd realized it meant he was thinking rings around her with hidden agendas, hidden thoughts, non-charitable thoughts masked by smiles.

Aargh!

"Mark?" Ronnie's father called out. "You have hereby been assigned the seat organization at the long table. A good test of your business management skills."

Ronnie rolled her eyes, but secretly whispered a prayer of thanks. Her dad was always springing surprise "tests" on his children, his wife, his guests. They were always benevolently offered and withdrawn at any sign of real discomfort, but even so, all too often in the last few years they'd been directed at Ronnie. Like he figured she needed a little more help than his other children in finding her direction.

Rather than shrink from the task, Mark stepped out of the crowd and led them all into what was often the Cleary table tennis room, location of many family tournaments growing up. Now, for the Christmas season, the table tennis topping had been removed from the massive old dining room table and a mixed collection of twelve chairs had been set up around it. The table top seemed to almost groan with pride under its cherry-colored table-cloth covered with the best plates, cutlery, and glasses, and her mother and Aunt Margery were just putting out the last of the dishes of food Ronnie had smelled earlier when she'd arrived.

The roast ham sat on a large white platter. There was a pitcher of water and two of eggnog, another of cranberry juice, and two bottles of red wine. The cookies were presumably still in the oven or out on the kitchen counter to cool off, but the smell of sugars and savories filled the room—baking and meat and pineapple glaze and mashed potatoes and peas and turnips and, beside the cooked carrots, something that looked suspiciously like a plum chutney. Which made Ronnie wonder what was in some of the covered dishes. Her mother rarely experimented in the kitchen, but when she did, the results could be…interesting.

Then Mark was directing seating assignments and her attention went completely from the food to him. With a calm confidence that showed he understood the Cleary's visiting ethic, he directed Ronnie's father to one end of the table and Ronnie's mother to the other (the end closer to the kitchen; no fool, he). He likewise separated Alex and Suzie but gave Nick the explicit permission to sit beside either of them if he chose.

"I want to sit beside Aunt Ronnie!" the kid declared

Mark pointed to a chair two down the right table end from Ronnie's father for Nick, then indicated the one left of that for Ronnie. Nick jumped into his chair. Ronnie nodded with a restrained smile and took the seat indicated, bemused as to whether Mark would seat himself in the empty chair to her left.

She had to wait through the remaining five assignments—splitting up Mr. and Mrs. Stephanopolus but putting them directly across from each other on either side of Ronnie's father, putting Aunt Margery beside Mr. Stephanopolus, Uncle Sean beside Mrs. Stephanopolus, Emma at Uncle Sean's other elbow. Ronnie grinned to see her ruddy-faced uncle very ostentatiously work that elbow over Emma's plate in the most obnoxious manner possible. Mrs. Stephanopolus looked on, horrified, while Emma delightedly stabbed her fork through Sean's sweater repeatedly until the man finally yelped and drew his elbow back to his side in mock affront.

And then there was only one seat left—to Ronnie's left.

She smiled inwardly as Mark, his task complete to the evident satisfaction (or at least tolerance) of everyone, pulled out the chair and sat down. Ha! She'd snagged him. Captured his eye. Tickled his fancy. Of course, he might just be a small-town guy going to Harvard, and she might be the only single female of marriageable age at the table, but Ronnie would take the ego boost where she could.

"Well done," Ronnie whispered to him and caught a relieved release of breath from him, too subtle for anyone but Ronnie to see. It was actually kind of endearing.

Then her father was indicating for everyone to join hands so they could sing grace, a simple tune sung, sung in rounds, that Ronnie had grown up with. She was impressed again as Mark caught on after just one time through. His parents contented themselves with smiling and nodding their heads in time. Ronnie focused hard on their faces and on everyone else around the table as they sang.

It kept her from blushing over the surprising tingle she got from the dry, strong fingers she felt holding her left hand.

2

OKAY, MARK THOUGHT as he fought to keep his focus on the sung Cleary family grace, this was unexpected.

When he'd flown home last month to check out his mother's hints about his father's health, a part of him had suspected it was all a bit of clumsy manipulation to get him to come back to Mayville after he got his MBA. If they'd only known the other forces pushing him in that same direction...

But his mother's worries had turned out to be legitimate, Mark found, when he took his dad's family doctor out for a beer and persuaded him into a pseudo-breach of doctor-patient confidentiality. Andreas had suffered not one, but two minor myocardial infarctions, i.e. heart attacks, which the doc was sure came from the stress of managing a house-construction business through the recession and slow recovery.

Without his son helping him along anymore, Mark heard him say silently.

So Mark had gone back to Harvard and made a phone call to accept the unusual proposition he'd turned down in September. It involved first finishing his MBA in the spring, then returning to Mayville to help the family business. Just when he'd thought he was finally out, just when he thought he'd finally have the same chance to fly that he'd given his younger siblings, he'd committed to coming back here for five to ten more years of purgatory. Nothing for him here. Nothing but obligation, duty…

Then this. The unexpected. Veronica Cleary. Now "Ronnie" to everyone.

Mark's memory of her as a kid was of a snotty little ginger girl who flipped so fast between her moods that he'd finally given up on her even though he'd found her fascinating. Besides, she'd been two years younger than him and his brothers would have ribbed him mercilessly if he'd even *looked* at her in high school.

But now? The snotty kid had grown into a redheaded knockout so sexy and…electric…that he could barely find the breath to sing with her left hand holding his. Her hand was hot like she was on fire inside. When she looked at him, there was almost a rage, a passion, *something*, that burned out of her eyes. Then she'd blush and look away and be all sweetness and light with everyone. Showing she was as confusing now as she had been as a kid.

The stupid thing was, as the dinner progressed he found himself falling into the same patterns around her as he had back then too. Show off. Paddle as fast he could. Dance and talk and show how brilliant he was. That was generally death, he knew, for any girl with half a brain. And yet here he went again…

~~~~

"No, the rebound won't take hold everywhere around the country," Mark said and gestured so broadly with his knife in his right hand, his fork in his left, that Ronnie had to sit back a bit to avoid getting hit. The doofus might have the looks of a short Greek god but he sure got worked up about things. Small town. None of Louis's big-city control.

"But here, it will!" his father called from across the table.

"Hear! Hear!" said Ronnie's dad.

"Yes, actually," Mark agreed. "Studies show it's already happening. Strong demand for high value homes in stable communities within two hours of a major city like Chicago. They can even become commuter towns, attract a whole new breed of businesses…"

Ronnie's dad humphed. "Which means hordes of people with money who aren't particularly invested in *this* community. Not what we want to have happen here."

"Slow and steady growth," Sean intoned in his best impersonation of his brother's occasional political pronouncements.

"A balancing act, like many things in life," Colin Cleary shot back.

"Minus the snowstorms, I wish," Ronnie's mother piped in.

"Not that I'd really want to be in Chicago during this one either," said Mark.

And suddenly all eyes were on Ronnie again. She blushed and put down her own knife and fork. "What? I *love* Chicago when it snows! You should see Chester's. It's like Santa's workshop, but better smelling."

"With prettier elves!" said Uncle Sean.

"Hunh?" said Nick, lifting his head from his mashed-potato-gravy lake at the mention of elves.

His timing was so spot on, the entire table cracked up. Then it hushed for a second as the blowing snowstorm which had whooshed over the town about fifteen minutes into their meal actually managed to make the house creak somewhere upstairs. The Cleary house was on the east edge of town, on a two-hundred foot wide property covered with trees, so there was almost a sense of being out in a dark forest.

Nick looked a little scared until his mother leaned forward and said, "You know what that is, don't you, Nicky?"

"What?" His eyes were wide.

"That's Santa whipping up the storm so there will be lots of snow on the rooftops for his sleigh to land on tomorrow night."

Nick's eyes went even wider, but with delight now. Which was like pouring gasoline on a fire when it came to Uncle Sean. The old scoundrel launched into an elaborate tale of all the untold truths about Santa Claus, that made him into some kind of Paul Bunyanesque super-being who reshaped not only the laws of physics but of space, time, and all western mythologies. Ronnie couldn't resist joining in. Nor could

Emma. Between the three of them, the tales got grander and more and more deranged until Nicky's eyes were almost popping out of their sockets, and everyone else around the table, even Mark's mother and father, were caught up in an unstoppable cascade of snorts and giggles.

At about the time Uncle Sean was describing Santa's global spy network of charmed piggy banks and stuffed animals which he used to tell whether boys and girls had been good, the front doorbell rang and almost no one seemed to hear it but Ronnie and her mom. Ronnie raised her chin and signaled she'd get it, wiped her mouth, and awkwardly slid and bumped her chair back from the table. She had to catch herself on Mark's shoulder as she did and, even though she was off-balance and weirdly giddy from Uncle Sean's stories, she got another little electric tingle from the contact. Real enough that Mark looked up, too, and caught her eyes. Smiling. Questioning.

Oh, please. Ego-stroking aside, that wasn't going anywhere. It would be just too stupid. Too much like a rebound romance. No, *exactly* like one. Pathetic. Common. And Ronnie Cleary was neither of those.

Mark turned back and Ronnie stumbled free of the table, heart beating hard, cheeks flushed. Fresh air. Reality.

And the front door. Right.

She was surprised to feel herself flushed and smiling foolishly as she left the dining room and made it out to the front hall. That, she guessed, just was what Christmas did to you. Christmas in the Cleary household, anyway. She refused to let it have anything to do with her surprise dinner companion, Mark Stephanopolus.

She gave her hair a quick back toss as she reached the front door, opened it...

And froze.

"Hey, Ron-Ron! Surprise!" said Louis, his arms wide, shoulders and head frosted with the blowing snow, his narrow square chin jutting out under his brilliant, bleached-white smile. A large Halston suitcase stood on the snow-covered front step beside him.

"Louis?" All the heady, good feeling of the moment before vanished in a confusing whirlwind of emotions as if the storm blew right through her. The hurt, the desire Louis still stirred in her, all the promises of their life together... "What are you—? How did you even get here? I was on the last train down."

Louis slapped his leather-gloved hands together and nodded over his shoulder at the curb where a bulky-looking SUV was slowly getting covered in snow. It looked like it would be covered within the hour. "Carl loaned me his Range Rover. I drove."

"You drove through this?" Ronnie had to raise her voice to be heard. The howling was getting fiercer, she realized. And she was freezing. Louis looked like he was turning a little blue himself.

"Can I?" he said, and pointed inside. He was only wearing

his black, calf-length Hugo Boss overcoat and short winter boots. Fine for Chicago, but totally inadequate if he'd gotten stranded somewhere out on the small highway coming down here. Foolish man. His vulnerability squeezed her heart.

So of course she waved him in. He grabbed his suitcase (way too big for just an overnight) and entered. Stomped and brushed the snow off himself as Ronnie closed the door behind him.

When she finally turned to look at him, she realized she had to fight to keep her voice even. "Why are you here, Louis?"

He flashed that super-masculine, confident smile at her. "What? A guy can't spend Christmas with his girlfriend?"

"I… The last time we talked…"

She let it die off as her father, obviously curious about what was taking her so long at the door, and who could possibly be calling on such a ridiculous night to be out, came loping down the hallway. His face got caught halfway between curiosity and a smile as he saw first who it was, then his daughter's face.

"Louis!" he said, cleared his throat and took in the suitcase. "Glad you could make it after all. Let me take your coat and you just go on into the dining room. We're almost ready for dessert, but I'm sure Evelyn can find you something to eat!"

"Thanks, Colin." Again the confident smile as he shrugged off his parka and handed it over. "I was just telling Ronnie here how that big software company merger closed a good week earlier than anticipated, so I borrowed the Range Rover from one of the other lawyers and managed to boot it out here after all. Couldn't miss a Cleary Christmas now, could I?"

"That's great." Colin eyed his daughter carefully. "Isn't that great, Ronnie?"

Ronnie was just…stunned, she realized. Was she *supposed* to still care this much? Or should she just be furious at him? Or triumphant that he'd come crawling back to her? It just… made no sense, Louis being here. Two weeks ago, she would have been simply over the moon with thankfulness that Louis was here, had obviously sacrificed a lot to be here, done everything he could to be by her side despite all the doubts she'd been having about his fidelity and interest in her. But that was before she'd gotten concrete proof of his cheating. That was before she'd confronted him and basically been told, point blank, that she should just accept it. That their relationship, Ronnie and Louis, had never had a realistic chance of working out. Their ambitions were too different. Their values. Louis knew where he was on his lifetime track. He knew exactly the high-flying corporate lawyer income and lifestyle he wanted out of life and he was well on the way to getting it. Ronnie, by contrast, barely seemed to know what she wanted for breakfast each morning. And her job in a sweets shop? That was just a joke. It was her avoiding a real career, a real life.

How did you love a person who could judge you like that? How could her heart, thumping now like a well-trained puppy tail, be so stupid?

"Let's…go in and introduce him to everyone he hasn't

met," Ronnie said.

Louis stepped up to her side and wrapped his arm around her, steering down the hall towards the dining room. "We'll talk later," he whispered into her ear.

We'd better," she said.

~~~~

Mark mentally shook his head. It was like Ronnie wanted to remind him all over again why he'd never pursued her as a child. One moment she was leaving the dinner table with a stumbling grab onto his shoulder and a smoldering look that had him wanting to jump up right then and wrap his hands around her tiny waist. The next she was traipsing back from the front door of the house with a handsome, sharp-faced guy in tow who was wearing a two thousand dollar suit and staying close enough to Ronnie's shoulder to establish ownership in the most obvious way possible.

And the way Ronnie leaned into *him*, the way her face was flushed, her steps shaky…

She introduced him as Louis, her boyfriend from Chicago. Everyone else seemed to know all about him. He could almost see Ronnie's mother blink her way through a mental readjustment and consciously reset her sights to focus on her daughter's best prospect. It made Mark feel about two feet tall and he wished he could just slide under the table and disappear.

But he didn't. Because that was just life, wasn't it? You were dealt a lot of confusing cards, some really amazing and some that just sucked, and it was up to you to figure out how you were going to play them.

So he smiled, stood, and greeted the newcomer, noting the lingering smell of an expensive cologne. Mark took a perverse satisfaction at the calculating, threatening look the guy gave him, held his gaze, then shifted his chair gracefully to the left to make room for Louis to sit between his girlfriend and Mark.

"Thank you," he said. "Really appreciate it." Educated voice. Of course it would be, given the suit. Stock broker, Mark guessed. Or lawyer. Maybe high-end sales. He had the smell of a shark on him.

"Not at all," Mark said and nodded towards Ronnie. "I can only take such beauty and wit in small doses."

Which made Ronnie go red once again, because she probably thought he was being sarcastic. Ha. It had even got her boyfriend coloring a bit. Even better.

Then Mark sat down and made a silent vow that he would drop it. Just be the gracious guest he'd planned to be, coming out tonight. He was really just here to support his mom and dad. The Lord knew he owed them at least this much.

Even so, the rest of dinner felt so surreal, with the howling wind outside and the smug Chicago stories Ronnie's boyfriend was recounting right at Mark's shoulder, that Mark could feel his resolution taking serious hits.

Then Louis turned his full attention on Mark's father, who was across the table from him down near the corner, and attacked in the one area that Mark himself felt compromised.

Louis asked Andreas about his current projects, but before Andreas had finished answering, nodded sagely and asked, "Have you ever considered partnering with a national building company, like Panderos Homes or Stanco Brothers?"

Ouch.

"No, I don't think so. No."

Of course his father hadn't. He'd fought that kind of approach his whole life and valued his independence.

"Because," Louis went on, "high end homes outside a major city are basically a dead end without some kind of economy of costs that you get with a nationwide sales approach."

"I don't think that is so," Andreas said, looking nervously at his son. Mark couldn't meet his eyes. Because it was Mark who'd convinced him, long before the Boston job offer, that he *could* proceed as he'd always done. And whatever plans Mark might have had for the future, he couldn't take those arguments back.

"It's true," Louis said. "There are tons of studies. These kinds of developments are always the slowest ones out of a recession. Always the most vulnerable in a weak recovery."

"Really?" Andreas said, looking increasingly unhappy. Calling on his son. *Calling* on him.

Fine.

"I'm curious," Mark piped up. "These studies you're talking about. Who did them?"

Louis blinked. Paused. "Lots of people. The National Industry and Building Association, for one."

"Right," Mark said. "The Grovenor Report. But that was done back in the eighties. Kind of a different situation with soaring interest rates and all, don't you think?"

"Not that different. I believe Stanco just released a report about this a couple months ago, too."

Mark chuckled, making Louis blink even harder. Obviously the blinking covered anger or discomfort. Good. "Sorry," Mark said. "Nothing against Stanco, and it's not really fair to you, either, because you've never seen the homes my father has built, have you?"

"What's your point?" Louis's voice was frosty enough to stop the separate conversation Sean, Emma, and Ronnie's mother were having at the other end of the table. Everyone was paying attention now. Mark saw that Ronnie was sinking slowly in her seat. Too bad. This particular thing wasn't about her.

"Stanco," Mark said, "makes cookie-cutter monster homes that are built on the fringes of rapidly growing commuter communities, often by clear-cutting hillsides or, down south, by draining swampland. My dad builds high-end custom homes that are carefully integrated into their environments, usually in neighborhoods in well-established smaller towns with independent industries."

Louis smiled thinly. A shark smile. Mark prepared himself.

"I think I heard someone mention you're still in school,

right?" Louis said now, simultaneously pointing out (wrongly) that Mark was younger and that he wasn't yet engaged in the real world of industry.

"I am in school, yes," Mark replied. Considered playing the Harvard card. Decided that was just puffery and not needed here.

Louis nodded. "I remember what that was like—a lot of professors who had little or no real world experience going on about what the people in the industry should have done or should now do to make things fit the professor's theory of how the world worked. I remember it was quite a shock when I got out, actually got down into the trenches with people doing real world deals, and heard them talk about how the real world never followed the experts' models. Am I right, Mr. Stephanopolus?"

Mark's dad looked flustered, being put on the spot, which was a pretty slimy tactic. But sharks used those, didn't they. Whatever worked.

Mark raised a hand. "It's okay, Pop. Let me." He swiveled in his seat to face Louis more directly. "Louis, I don't want to get into a…um…urination match over who has the most real-world experience in the area of actually building and selling homes because this is a holiday dinner and you're the very lucky boyfriend of the host's eldest daughter. Let's just say we disagree over the prospects of my father's business and whether he should partner with people like Phillip and Edward Stanco, both of whom I've met personally, by the way."

"As have I!" Louis blurted.

"Great. So we've both met them and can testify that they're nice guys. Can we leave it at that?"

Mark saw Louis's chest and chin rising. There was absolutely no way he was going to leave it there. Well fine. Mark could feel his own blood rising and welcomed it. He'd had enough of holding back around such people. Let Chicago Boy bring it!

But suddenly Ronnie had grabbed Louis's right arm. "Truce!" she said. "And now, Mom, I think we're just about all ready for the dessert we've been smelling for the last hour. Can I and Louis help you serve it?"

It was Ronnie's mother's turn to look put on the spot. But only for a breath. Then she jumped up and said, "Certainly! Emma, Alexander, and Nick, would you please help clear?"

Louis caught Mark's eye. He was pissed. Would have liked to have another go at the punk who challenged him. And stay away from the girl!

Mark just shook his head. Whatever, Big City. She's too much work for this small town boy anyway.

~~~~

Thank goodness for dessert!

Consisting of both pecan and cherry pies as well as Christmas shortbread cookies and vanilla ice cream, this final course was involving enough that Ronnie saw Louis gradually ease back from the all-out battle he was so clearly eager to enter into with Mark.

And how would that battle have gone? Ronnie had seen Louis rip apart a waiter who'd given them rude service once. He'd pursued the matter all the way up the chain to the owner of the hotel in which the restaurant was situated and gotten the young man fired. And he'd told stories of undermining and humiliating opponents to his business deals. Ronnie wasn't sure she *liked* that side of Louis, but she still found it exciting. It was so different from the males she'd grown up with. So filled with raw masculinity. The kind of unselfconscious drive you needed to really thrive in a place as rough as Chicago.

But here? An all-out battle would be kind of horrifying. Particularly if—and here, the thought gave her a guilty thrill—Louis lost this one.

She looked left to see Louis attacking his piece of pecan pie, and Mark, more thoughtful, digging into his own slice of cherry. Mark caught her eye and raised a fork, as if to say, *You're right. Dessert stops all wars.* Or maybe it was just, *Good pie.*

Either way, Ronnie smiled back. This kind of dessert was indeed sustenance against the howling storm outside. It was balm for the work-driven soul in a way that a good website could never be. It was a sugar-laden doorway to the sort of Christmas torpor that, Ronnie reflected, could easily lead you into that great secular symbol of the holiday, a red-nosed jolly man with a huge midsection that quaked and shook like a bowlful of jelly. All right with the world. Everyone jolly and at peace. Louis fully occupied.

Ronnie didn't want it to end.

But it did.

Because of the storm, Uncle Sean and Margery were ordered to stay over. Mark, after a quick check on the conditions of his father's Ford Super Duty, said he'd have no trouble driving his folks home. There was a brief awkwardness at the door when he leaned forward to give Ronnie a "Nice to have met you" kiss and she intercepted it with a still-electric handshake. Basic biology, Ronnie had concluded. Simple animal attraction. You didn't have to read anything more into it.

And her awkwardness with it was completely forgotten in the awkwardness that came after the Stephanopoluses had left. Ronnie's mother, without consulting her, chirpily announced that since Louis was there, he and Ronnie would be staying in the downstairs guest room.

Because it had a double bed.

Thanks, Mom. You got progressive right when I finally wished you weren't.

The one blessing was that, since Ronnie had assumed she'd be sleeping solo and knew her parents liked to keep the house frosty cold at night, she'd packed her long flannel nightgown. And once she'd brushed her teeth and had a quick shower before bed, she put it on with absolutely no intention of taking it off, that night or any other when Louis was around. Not, at least, until she'd worked through this confusing swirl of feelings she had towards him.

He was sitting in bed with his back propped up against the bed's headboard when Ronnie came in. He clicked off his smartphone where he'd no doubt been answering e-mails, and gave her an appreciative smile.

Ronnie stepped into the room, closed the door behind her and didn't go any closer. "So talk," she said.

"That Stephanopolus guy was something, hunh? Not a frigging clue what he's talking about."

Ronnie said nothing.

"So what?" Louis shrugged. "I was late in trying to find a way to come to Christmas with your parents. I got here, though, didn't I? No harm. No foul."

"Our last conversation was you giving me two weeks to find a new place to live while you'd be staying with Vivienne."

"Yeah. That." He ducked his head and took a long breath. "I broke up with Vivienne."

"Why?"

"Isn't that obvious, Ronnie? I realized I'd been a jackass. I'm in love with you. I always have been."

She fought to keep off her face how that made her heart jump. Even now. Even after all he'd said to her. "Is that supposed to be an apology?"

He blinked. "That's supposed to be a…I don't know…how about…the whole argument we had? It should never have happened. What I said about you not being good enough, or career-focused enough, to be with me—that was stupid."

"You think?" His casualness about it... Didn't he know how he'd absolutely devastated her with his words? Was he truly that blind?

"So?"

"So? What do you expect me to do here, Louis? You cheated on me and then tried to make me feel like it was somehow my fault for not being good enough. Am I supposed to just forget all of that? Am I supposed to take you back?"

Louis looked down at his hands, almost sheepish? Then he looked up again and Ronnie saw the one thing that she never thought she would. Something that actually made her rethink her half-formed plan to kick Louis to the curb first thing tomorrow morning so she could get enough distance from him to actually let the wounds of her heart heal over.

Louis's eyes were wet. And Louis was not a crier. Ronnie thought she'd seen him tear up maybe three times in the two years they'd been together—once when his dad died and a couple times in movie theaters where she was pretty sure he thought no one had noticed.

"You're right, Ronnie. I can't expect that. Can't ask it. All I can do is ask you, beg you really, to just listen for a moment and maybe understand. My job... It's harder than I make it out to be. There's been a lot of stress. I've made some mistakes I haven't told you about that could have gotten me fired. So this thing with Vivienne... I was too ashamed to talk to you. With you I always wanted to be perfect. With her I didn't have to be because she *knew* how much I'd screwed up and wanted me anyway, so… Like I said, it was stupid. Stupid to start. Stupid to keep it going. And when I attacked you, that was stupidest of all. That was my shame talking. Just looking at you each day… You're always so good, so honest, so straight up. Everything I couldn't be."

"Louis…"

"Even coming out here!" he cut her off. "That was me trying to bluff my way back to you. And I'd understand if you raised your bullshit meter and called me on it. Kicked me out. But I'm asking you, begging you here, to please just give me a chance. Give me this Christmas to make it right. I don't know, really, exactly how I'd be able to go on without you. It took being stupid enough to drive you away, I think, for me to realize that."

"I…"

"You loved me enough once to talk about wanting us to get married. Just give me a chance to prove I'm still the guy you'd want to do that with."

"I'm…" She paused but he just waited this time, his wet eyes watching hers anxiously. And she felt her heart flip over for him. She'd fallen deeply in love with the sharp, masculine, powerful man Louis had been. She had to know, deep down, that so much virility had to include a certain amount of blindness, emotional stupidity. But if he loved her enough to actually push his way through all the bluffing and bluster like this, to say he actually needed her…

"Just a week," she said. "Until New Year's, if you have that long off."

His face had burst into an unabashed, ear-to-ear smile. "I have as long as it takes. My whole life."

Ronnie held up a hand. "Until New Year's. And…you'll be sleeping on the floor. I'll get you some extra bedding."

Then she was out the door, leaning back against it and breathing hard. And tears were suddenly flowing hotly down her cheeks as she thought of Mark, and dessert, and the Chicago dream life she'd had and lost and was being offered again. Her breath hitched painfully in her chest and he put a hand there.

Was this the pain of intense relief, or the pain of someone ripping the barely-formed scab off a wound that had just been starting to heal? And if she couldn't tell the difference, what did that say?

3

FOR MARK, driving home found him uncharacteristically torn between different obsessions. First, triggered again by the brief handshake she'd used to block his goodbye kiss on the way out the door, was a whirl of thoughts about Ronnie. Despite declaring to himself that he had no intention of pursuing her, everything about her seemed to be stuck in his brain like a brightly-colored movie reel that came complete with touch and smell and sound. Completely unavailable and completely captivating. It made no sense to him. A mystery.

Before he could puzzle over that for long, however, his attention was back on his father. The old man sat in the passenger seat, looking like he was going to give himself another heart attack or a stroke. He clutched and re-clutched the shoulder strap of his seatbelt and muttered under his breath, "Studies show...ha!...never going to recover...never going to work...never worked like me his whole life..."

In the rear of the Super Duty cab, Mark's mother, Antonia, a diminutive dark-haired woman who'd grown up on the Island of Mykonos before meeting Mark's father on a summer holiday, marrying him and moving to America, first to Vermont, then to Illinois, bearing three sons along the way, kept trying to lean far enough forward to massage her husband's shoulders as she reassured him over and over, "It's going to be alright, Dreas. It's going to be fine."

It made Mark wish for a moment that Ronnie hadn't interfered with Louis back there at the dinner table. Mark really would have liked to have taken that creep down a peg or two. Nothing physical. Just a good old-fashioned battle of intellects and willpower, the sort of thing Mark had been winning since he was old enough to talk. It probably would have horrified most of the assembled guests, including Mark's parents and particularly Ronnie.

It still would have been nice.

It also might have taken his mind off this choice he'd made to come back to his father's business after he graduated. Both because it felt like he'd be putting his life on hold, and he wouldn't be coming to it with clean hands. He'd be bringing a secret agenda. Lying to his dad by omission, which was not his style. Had never been his style.

Damn it!

It shot such a bolt of guilt through him that he wobbled the steering wheel, making the huge beast of a pickup he was driving weave drunkenly on the snowed streets, the tires spitting snow sideways with a roar and barely holding their traction.

"Marcario!"

"Sorry, Mom!"

And he straightened out the wheels, gasping in the still-sharp winter air in the cab as everything popped in line again. Wished he could straighten out his life as easily. Go back to the guy he'd been growing up, when everything was simple. You did your chores at home, you worked hard at school, you learned how to handle a saw and nail gun in your spare time. And if girls made it really *really* clear that they liked you, maybe you even went out to the occasional movie at one of the town's two cinemas. Then he'd graduated, gotten a quick degree in business, and gone back to join his dad in Gold Construction for a few years, working his way from the construction and estimates end up into managing worksites and smaller projects.

But then somewhere in those years after college, he'd gotten itchy or something. Needed more. Needed different. So, almost on a whim, he'd taken his GMATs and cobbled together some references for the application to Harvard. Almost cried when he'd gotten in and his pop had told him, with tears in his eyes, that he was so proud a son of his could do such a thing. That he'd financially support Mark through his degree. No strings. Because that's what a parent did—give when they could.

And now? Would he be proud of Mark now, if he knew what Mark had agreed to?

Would Ronnie?

He blinked as he surprised himself with that thought, and almost drove by their street.

Ronnie.

Hunh.

There was that offbeat idea again—him and Ronnie.

"Marcario, why you laughing so much?" said his mother. "You think this is funny?"

"What's funny? What is funny?" joined in his father, at least pulling him out of his angry muttering.

And Mark wanted to say, *How could you not know? Didn't you see her? Face round as a valentine with the same sort of delicious curves below. Wild hair in a frizzy bright orange that made him want to smooth it down, feel it curl and stretch under his fingers.*

"Nothing, Mom. Nothing, Pop. Almost home. You feeling okay, Pop?"

But his lips, he knew, were still turned up as he let himself think, stupidly, about Ronnie's eyes. So green sometimes that they caught the light like an emerald, but almost stormy when he actually looked into them. Like they were filled with storm clouds and burning pitch. It was probably all his imagination, but he swore he could see the turbulence of her heart and thoughts in them and couldn't imagine how any one person could contain so much turmoil.

Maybe he liked them so much because they put his own struggle of conscience in perspective. He'd always lived, even more than his parents, with such clear rules of right and wrong, do or not do. Now he was growing up and finding that there were lots of times when the rules were not clear and the path was uncertain.

He suspected that Ronnie had learned that lesson a lot earlier than him. Maybe way back in first grade when he, two years older, was still trying to impress her by paddling as fast as he could.

So what? Should he consult with her about which sucky life option he should take careerwise right now?

He turned into his parents' wide driveway behind a truck already parked there and beside one of the two parked SUVs, and he smiled to himself. Advice from someone that changeable? That would be…interesting. It would be almost certainly wrong for Mark, given that Ronnie obviously lived her life in a whole other mental and emotional headspace than Mark.

They were so wrong for each other that it was actually humorous.

But yeah, whatever she had to tell him (if he ever revealed his true career plan to her, which almost certainly would never happen) would be…interesting.

4

E VEN WITH THE LATE NIGHT CLEAN-UP after the guests left, Ronnie was up by six the next morning. Habit. That rising hour usually let her get downtown by seven in Chicago, missing most of the mad morning rush and getting enough of a lead on making fresh batches of candy and treats at Chester's. She'd never understood the taste difference you got in same day-sweets, even hard candies, before she'd worked there. Now she was as fanatic about it as Rolf. They made an incredible team.

But was that really enough? She loved it but…for all Louis saying he'd been stupid, she knew he'd been saying what he really thought serious when he'd called her job a hobby, not a career choice.

For some reason, Mark's face rose in her mind, munching on her candy and shaking his head in disbelief over Louis's assessment.

But what Mark would never understand, she thought with a quick shake of her head, what she was almost scared to admit to herself, was that Louis might have been right—

you couldn't make a real career out of making candy. And maybe Ronnie had always known it. Which was part of why she'd been drawn in so quickly by Louis when she met him. Because Louis clearly was en route to the kind of exciting, big city success that Ronnie had always dreamed of. And he had a conscience—she'd met him at a charity fundraiser, after all—so it wasn't just about the money. It was about his energy. His drive. His desire to go big. If she went with him, she'd have that energy too...*even if her candy making didn't work out.*

How could she even explain that to someone content to live and work in a small town like Mayville?

And how could she explain the devastation she'd felt when she'd lost all that promise? The intense need she had to turn back to it and see if it could work after all?

She pushed Mark's face out of her head and looked instead at Louis's passed-out form on the pile of blankets and single pillow on the floor where she'd made him sleep. So peaceful and handsome and innocent-looking when asleep. Like the man she'd always thought he could be with just a little gentling from her. All his strength with just a little bit of female civilizing.

Fighting off a sudden and powerful desire to drop down and snuggle with him on the blankets—that would *not* let her testing period for him be a test at all—she grabbed her clothes for the day and slipped past his sleeping form to shower and change in the downstairs bathroom.

When she finally made it out to the kitchen, she found her

dad was already there, making his special porridge. Her mom came in just a few minutes later. Then Nick. Then, maybe because she'd sensed just how intensely she'd been thinking about him, Louis.

He bopped in, looking his bright, handsome, arrogantly charming self, and proceeded to join Ronnie's mom in her massive bacon-and-egg making production process for everyone else. By ten, everyone was up and either eating breakfast, finishing, or cleaning up. The day had swung around 180 degrees to freezing, brilliant sunshine with nary a breeze. Almost as if the storm had blown all the bad stuff through the town and out.

Except it had left chest high snow drifts everywhere that made Uncle Sean groan as he looked out to his poor little Taurus. The car showed as no more than a bump in the line where the driveway used to be.

"Now don't you mind there, boyo," said Ronnie's dad, clapping an arm over his younger brother's shoulders. The plow'll be by shortly and then we'll all help to shovel you out. Right, Louis?"

Louis looked up, obviously startled, but covered it with a grin. "Of course we will! Partnership! Working together! Great things accomplished!"

Ronnie thought of Louis's pathetic winter gear and rolled her eyes.

But sure enough, barely fifteen minutes later, the snowplow came down their street, heaping a good seven-foot high ridge of white across the end of their driveway as it passed. And twenty minutes after that, all the men plus Ronnie and Emma were outside, grunting and sweating as they shoveled mounds of snow off Uncle Sean's Taurus, Alex's CR-V, and Emma's Prius (which at least had winter tires).

When they got back inside an hour later, everyone was wiped and thinking about hot showers, but Ronnie's mom had already begun preparing lunch and had hot apple cider waiting. Then, as Ronnie was about to doff her boots and grab some cider and a chair close to the stove, her mother tagged her on the shoulder.

"Dear, could you drive the pickup downtown to the Dover Pantry for me? There are a few fresh things I need for Christmas dinner tomorrow that I forgot to get."

"I… Sure." Ronnie shrugged her winter coat back on with a groan.

Louis stepped forward to her elbow. "I'll go with her."

"Actually," Ronnie's father said before Ronnie could tell Louis she'd rather do the Mayville re-familiarization on her own, "I was hoping you and Emma's boyfriend, Jeff, could help me split some logs for a bit out back. We're running a bit short of firewood after everything we blazed through last night."

It was a bad lie, but Ronnie suspected her dad sensed her need to get away, and maybe also valued having another lawyer to chat about things with for a change. How Jeff, a radiologist, would fit into that conversation, she didn't know. But Jeff was

Emma's boyfriend, so that was for Emma to worry about.

Besides, maybe having two small-town professionals working with Louis would be a good start on the gentling process. Infuse a little bit of the kinder, slower Mayville pace that Ronnie didn't want to *live* in, but was gradually understanding might not be a bad thing to carry inside her. And maybe a bit in Louis too.

She grabbed the list and the keys to her dad's Toyota pickup truck from her mother and headed to get her coat and boots.

~~~~

The Dover Pantry lay in the Bark Street Mall, just off Main Street.

Basically a group of nine shops cheek-to-jowl together with their own parking lot, today it was bounded on either end with huge, plowed-up snowbanks and already full of cars and trucks. The stores included a Wool Barn, a small Staples, a Lightyear Electronics, a gift card shop, a Molly's Books, a shoe store, and a men's and women's clothing store and a pub—why do your last-minute Christmas shopping anywhere else?

The Dover Pantry, the closest thing the mall had to a grocery store, was a farmers' market with European spices, sausages, and chutneys. One step inside and Ronnie was yanked right back to her childhood and her first love affair with food, in this case with spicy pepperoni rings. How she'd traveled from that to computers and websites then to sweets was a convoluted journey indeed.

"Veronica! Is good to see you! *Merviglioso!*"

It was Beppe Mamazza, the same sweet little white-haired guy who'd been running the Pantry for at least as long as Ronnie could remember, though she'd never quite understood his reasoning for naming it after a British landmark.

"Hi Beppe. Just picking up a few things for my mom." She tugged off her gloves and fished out her mother's list.

He clucked his tongue and set off around the store, pulling things off the shelves and out of the produce shelves for her. "I hear so much about you this morning," he said as he went, "and now here you are!"

"So much about me? I only got in last night."

"Yes, yes. I know. But one night is all it takes, *cara mia!* Ka-boom! The love, she hits!"

"'The love'? What are we talking about here, Beppe?" But her fickle heart, she was annoyed to find, already suspected. It had doubled its tempo.

"The young man! The other wanderer, yes? But he comes home so much more than you. He says he gonna stay home soon, yes? As soon as he finish his studies."

Which pretty much confirmed it. "You're talking about Mark Stephanopolus?"

"Marcario, yes! He talk on and on and on about how beautiful you are, how smart, how funny, how very...you know..." He made a curving gesture over his thin little body and waggled his hips so that Ronnie had to laugh.

"Okay, now I *know* you're pulling my leg. Was he really in here?"

Beppe nodded.

"And what did he say about me? Really."

Beppe shrugged. "He ask how long you going to stay here in town."

Ronnie blushed. "He and his folks were over at my parents' house for dinner when I got in last night."

Beppe peered at her closely then pointed a finger at her nose. "You see? One night is all it takes. Ka-boom!"

Still blushing, Ronnie shook her head. "Tell that to my boyfriend, Louis. He got in last night, too."

Beppe waved his hand. "Oh yes. I hear about him too."

"From Mark?"

"From him, yes. It do not sound to me like you and him, the Louis, are a 'good fit.'"

"Really. That's what you got from Mark, hunh?" She would have slammed her fist into her palm if it hadn't been so clichéd. "Since I'm going to be here all week, I think I might just have to talk to that boy."

Beppe smiled. "He is looking in the zippy-zappy store."

"The electronics store? Here in the mall?"

"That's where he say he was going about ten minutes ago."

Forcing her racing heart to slow, Ronnie nodded. "Okay. Did you find everything on my mom's list?"

"All, yes. Forty-seven, sixty-two."

Ronnie nodded, paid, donned her gloves again, and took

the bag. Then she hurried out of the store, turned right, and into Lightyear Electronics. Mark was standing in front of the video game rack. He didn't look at her as she walked over to stand beside him, but she could feel the electricity crackle like he'd been rubbing his feet on a carpet somewhere, just waiting to shock her.

"So do I buy for what my two older nephews will like or what their parents want them to like?" he said, studying the racks intently.

"Meaning what? Blood-and-guts action versus…?"

"Puzzle games. I don't know."

"Sister's kids or brother's?"

"You don't remember?"

Ronnie pursed her lips. "We only took swimming together. I was a little kid and mostly trying not to drown."

"I've only got brothers. Two older and one younger. Two of them have sons, eleven and twelve. The third has a young boy and a girl."

"And how were you all raised? To be all proper and polite like you are now?"

Mark laughed, but still didn't look at her. That was starting to grate on her nerves, something to which he seemed completely oblivious as he said, "My dad had us out learning to hunt and set snares for rabbits by the time I was five."

"Your father, Andreas? I always figured him more for the, um, growing grapes and making his own wine kind of guy."

Mark laughed again. "That too, but there was definitely

a wild kind of frontiersy streak that he passed on to... Hm. I guess I just answered my own question about what my brothers would want for their kids, hunh?" He quickly scooped up two titles labeled Teen, and a third that looked like a racing game.

He *finally* turned and looked at her. And damn if his liquid brown eyes didn't actually sparkle in the late morning light. At least, Ronnie was gratified to see, his irises visibly dilated as he took her in, his gaze traveling all over her face and quickly up and down her body.

"Thank you," he said, which somehow seemed to be just for her being there, for letting him breathe in her essence.

Ronnie licked her lips, but managed to stop herself from brushing back her hair with her gloved hand. "Don't do that," she said.

"Do what?"

"Look at me like that."

"Like what?"

Ronnie blushed so hard she could feel it prickle her scalp. "Like you think you've got some kind of chance with me. Like maybe the fact that we both grew up here somehow entitles you to a shot. I'm not some kind of wild deer or rabbit you can hunt down or snare *or* seduce."

The corner of his mouth quirked up. "Your mother said you weren't engaged to Louis yet."

"At least we haven't announced it yet." Oh, you liar. Lying by implication. Had she learned that from Louis? Her father would be so proud. Not.

"Are you?"

"What?"

"Engaged. You're not wearing an engagement ring."

Her jaw dropped at his audacity and she held up her hands. "I'm *wearing* gloves."

"You weren't last night. And I would think the eldest daughter, coming home for Christmas, would have been pretty excited to show off an engagement ring if she had one."

"Maybe we don't do things like that in Chicago. This isn't some old Frank Capra movie."

"Ha. Look around you. Mayville is exactly like an old Capra movie."

"What? *It's a Wonderful Life*? Where the Christmas angel proves how it's better to sacrifice everything to stay in the little box you were born in?"

"Ooh, nasty. But I was actually thinking more of *It Happened One Night*. Feisty heroine who's not so happy with her rich fiancé. She heads off into small town America and inadvertently finds her true love."

"Who's a boastful, con artist reporter who lies to her over and over until she runs away from him."

"Hm. Okay. How about *Sweet Home Alabama*?"

"Jumping directors, eras, and entire plot styles now. You're getting desperate."

He shrugged and somehow looked like a vulnerable little boy for a second. Simply real. No dramatic tears like Louis had (so conveniently?) shed last night. Just a naked desire to be liked. The effect was so unexpected and heart-tugging that Ronnie actually swayed back and had to put a hand on the display rack near the window to steady herself.

"Have to confess I'm not the best at the quick repartee," he said. "Not great at the whole schmoozing thing they try to teach us is so critical in business."

And now she found herself grinning stupidly at him (*Stop it!*) as she said, "Oh, I'm pretty sure you do okay in that area."

"No, really. I was taught to wrestle for things I wanted growing up. Two older brothers. They still make fun of me when I talk about liking chick flicks."

"Whereas they like that kind of knowledge in Harvard? Are you trying to pretend you're not some kind of carefully-concealed genius brain? We all heard you argue with Louis last night. What the others don't know is that may be the first time Louis has been put in his place in an argument in years."

He shrugged again but held her gaze. "Like I said. I was taught to wrestle for things I want."

Ronnie blushed again and shook her head. "I have to get these groceries home to my mother. She'll be getting anxious. She had lunch almost ready when I left."

"Okay. It's a small town. I'm sure I'll see you around. Very soon, in fact."

"Um…I don't think coming to the house would be a good idea."

"I agree. It's why you'll be coming to me."

And before she had a chance to demand exactly what

he meant by that, he turned from her to take his nephews' Christmas gifts up to the cash register. Ronnie fumed for just a moment, then turned on her heel herself and headed out the door.

Like she, newly rejoined by a man who was everything she supposedly wanted in the world, would go chasing some childhood acquaintance she'd just met. Re-met? Mark might be brighter than Louis when arguing business development, and even more solidly masculine in a salt of the earth kind of way, but he was also right up there with Louis in arrogance too. *You'll be coming to me?*

Dream on, buddy.

5

Now was that, Mark wondered, fate or playing the probabilities of pre-Christmas shopping in a small town?

Either way, he couldn't stop smiling as he drove his father's Super Duty back from the mall with the gifts he'd brought for his nephews. And he knew the cause was Ronnie. Knew with a simple certainty that the answer to his life, or at least a key part of the answer, was her. Despite everything he'd been thinking last night about them being so wrong for each other. Despite her protestations and possibly very real commitment she already had with Louis What's-his-face. The simple fact was that there was something about the two of them that clicked. He felt it and he knew, from her blushing, that she felt something too.

And because of that, he figured he *did* have a decent chance at getting her.

Or should he say winning her? Convincing her?

Any way he put it seemed to trivialize it somehow. Because she was right. She wasn't some kind of game animal or prize to be won. But he *was* going to court her. Carefully. The only way you could with someone so complicated.

And maybe somewhere along the way, he'd work through these other issues he'd taken on so that he'd actually be worthy of...of...being with her.

"Never going to be simple with her," he muttered to himself as he turned down Andrews Road and slowed to turn into his parent's wide-but-crowded driveway. As he pulled to a stop, his cell phone buzzed.

He pulled it out, saw the caller lack of caller ID, and went colder inside. But he clicked to answer it anyway. "Mark here."

"So how's the project looking?" said the voice of Edward Stanco on the other end of the line. Because Mark had only been telling half the truth when he'd told Louis at the table last night that he'd met Phillip and Edward Stanco. He'd not only met them. He'd petitioned them. He'd sat down with them. He'd agreed to come back to work for Gold Construction at least partly because of them.

"It's good," Mark answered now. "My father's work is always good. He only hires the best. Works with the best."

"Implication being that we're not."

"'Best' does have that connotation. It's an English word meaning kind of thing."

Stanco chuckled. "Except that you can be the best at one kind of thing, or in one area, and not be the best in another, wouldn't you say?"

"What are you claiming? You're the best at having lots of money?"

Again the chuckle, but it was a little forced now. "That would be us. And it would be the reason you agreed to scout out this deal for us, right, Mark? Or should I say Marcario? Or would you like Mr. Stephanopolus?"

By the end of it, the voice practically dripped with condescension, which Mark knew was a deliberate tactic to push his emotional buttons. It made him easier to manipulate. It had certainly worked back in Boston, when Stanco had invited him, with a carefully-worded invitation sent on Stanco Bros. blue-and-gold embossed letterhead, to a sit-down discussion of his future prospects. The voice had money, power, prestige, and a large number of high-level building opportunities to dangle in front of Mark as lures.

All of which he'd still managed to turn down until his father's heart attacks had demanded he go back to work at Gold Construction anyway.

And what Edward Stanco had outlined for him had sounded pretty innocuous, after all. "Scouting" he'd called it. "Spying" might have been more accurate. But it wasn't spying in order to underbid or otherwise take away business from GC. It was to examine this Putter's Ridge development GC was doing and find ways for Stanco to work their way into it. Ironically sort of what Louis himself had suggested. In return, if they did find a way to partner, Mark would take on an intermediary role, gradually transitioning into management in the larger Stanco organization.

The key was that if forming a working partnership

between Gold and Stanco did *not* work out, Mark would still have an in at Stanco. All he had to do then was get someone good enough to replace him that his father could still run GC without having to do everything himself.

All the reasons seemed to make sense back in Boston. Even more when he took the Red Line back to Harvard Square and walked across the Charles River to Allston just before the end of classes pre-Christmas. Because while Harvard tried to pretend its students came from every class and culture, the reality of the tuition fees and admissions process stacked the place with the sons and daughters of some of the wealthiest movers and shakers on Wall Street and other centers of finance around the world, plus men and women who'd already run their own consultancies or worked at high levels of finance. Amongst them, Mark had felt like a presumptuous country hick.

It was the immigrant mentality thing.

True, Mark was second generation. And he hadn't grown up poor. His father had always managed to provide an above-average lifestyle and education for his four sons, even when times were bad and Gold Construction was struggling. But Andreas Stephanopolus had always been, and would always be in his own mind, a struggling immigrant. He was the first of his family to come to America, the first of his family to send his children to university, the first to even learn English.

And deep down, Mark knew, Andreas would always fear that everything he'd achieved, everything he'd accomplished, could vanish overnight. During the recession, it almost had. He'd had to let two full-time staff go. He'd had to cancel two projects and draw out of the bidding on a third. On top of which he'd shelled out a hundred thousand for his third son to go and attend a business school that would supposedly guarantee Mark a solid career anywhere in corporate America.

So Mark had to *succeed*, even while he deep-down feared he could not.

Another reason to at least *explore* how GC might partner with Stanco. So why did he get a deep chill every time he actually talked to the Stanco CEO?

"I can tell you this much already," Mark said. "There are no guarantees that the Putter's Ridge project is going to fly."

"It doesn't have to *fly*, Mark. That's old thinking. It just has to carry itself and reinforce the company's goodwill. Get the town council used to the idea of Gold Construction doing value-added developments that push the city codes a little."

"My dad's been doing that for years."

"No, he's been rebuilding on tear-down sites or using subdivisions and rezonings. And before that it was mostly renovations. I read the paper you just turned in on it. All about sustainability and fitting in, right? Generating trust in the community."

"That was a by-product of the approach. Not why he did things that way."

"But it's the by-product we're most interested in. You had to have figured that out going in, kid. And this time the good will's going to attach to you. So when you find the way to bring us in, you'll already have their ear. You'll have shown them that this kind of thing's a very nice train ride for everyone involved. When town councils figure that out, bigger developers finally cut through their head-in-the-dirt blockades that are just killing Middle America."

"Or I could just graduate, take over as the head of Gold Construction when my dad retires, and keep this town tight-knit and close to the land the way it's always been."

There was a long silence on the other end of the line.

Finally Edward Stanco's voice said, "Yeah. You could do that. Of course you realize that you'd then become a hard competitor and when we come in, we'd simply wipe out Gold completely. Only difference is that it would take a little longer and, at the end of it, you'd be gone rather than having a shot at the big leagues. But you know what? It's totally your choice."

"Yes, it is," Mark said, fighting to keep his voice even. "It's what we agreed to. I never *committed* to—"

"Oh, don't be a fucking child, Stephanopolus. Of course you did. Your eyes got round with dollar signs. But you know what? Let's pretend you didn't. Let's pretend it was just me who heard you say you could make this happen. On the basis of which, I've been negotiating a deal with Woodwand that's going to determine if they bring their business and money to your little burg or somewhere else. Difference between your crap hometown booming in its own right or just becoming a commuter community."

"Woodwand international?"

"Meeting him January two. Which means I need a clear signal from you by then about whether there's a way you can get me a joint building deal with Gold."

"In nine days? With everyone on holidays?"

"Hey, how many people do you really need to talk to? One. Your dad. If you get him on board, even a clear intent to explore the possibility with me, I'll consider you've done your part of the deal. Okay?"

Mark's hands had gone tight on the phone. "It's not that simple. I've barely been part of the business for the last sixteen months. I have to be able to give him a solid business plan."

"You little…" Mark heard a muffled fumbling that could have been Stanco covering his phone while he swore or kicked something, then the man came back on with his voice tighter and meaner than Mark had ever heard it. "Okay, listen. I'm making allowances for the fact you come from a small town in the Midwest. I came from one myself. I get it, the whole careful-careful thing. But look, kid. This is how big, serious business deals are done. They've got real-world deadlines and need real-world results."

"I understand that, but—"

"No. No you don't. I offered you a deal to go and get something simple for me—a way for Stanco to get in on this project you're building with your dad on Putter's Ridge. A foot in the door. That's all. And now that you're home in the company of people with small vision, you're getting cold feet."

"I just—"

"So I'm giving you a little more incentive. I happened to be talking to the dean of your business school lately, being one of the school's more notable alumni, and mentioned your name. You know what he told me? They're considering giving you an award when you graduate. Yeah, you've really impressed them. But what do you think would happen if I told them that most of the ideas in the paper you just turned in for your mid-term grade, the one about sustainability and all, all came from one of *my* early unpublished papers that I gave you a copy of the first time you came to interview with me?"

"What the— You've got to be kidding me. Every example I cited came from my work with Gold Construction."

"Yeah. You plagiarized my work and modified it just enough to make it look like yours."

"Really?"

"Sorry, kid. I like you. I really do. It's why I went with you on this. But I repeat: I've made some serious plans based on your coming through, so I need you to come through. Either that or kiss your hundred-thousand-dollar Harvard MBA goodbye, along with any hopes of working anywhere other than your dad's business. And maybe not even there when I let slip to him what you agreed to do behind his back."

"Hunh. You really are one son of a bitch."

"See?" said Stanco. "Now that's why I like you. No fear. No simple capitulation. You just call it like you see it. And that's why your dad, and eventually the town council of Mayville and any other town council is going to like whatever you put to them. Because you're so damn trustworthy. And the crazy thing is, this *is* the right thing to do, kid. Once you let the eggnog settle, you'll see again that it's a no-brainer."

"Sure it is."

"Merry Christmas."

Stanco hung up.

Mark lowered his cell phone to his lap and stared at it for a good two minutes before he pocketed it and climbed out of the truck.

~~~~

Back in the Cleary kitchen, Ronnie reflected that this kind of hearty midwinter meal—harvest pumpkin-curry soup, and a spread of freshly baked whole-grain buns, sliced deli meats, cheese, pickles, tomatoes, and condiments to make your own sandwiches with, plus lots of cut-up fresh veggies and dip on the side—was exactly what had driven her into the food industry to begin with.

Food to fill the body and soul.

This lunch might not be sweets, she sighed as she wriggled her bum deep into the solid oak chairs around the kitchen table, but the crusty goodness of her honey ham, cucumber, and mustard creation had its own kind of divinity in the food pantheon.

The only speck of imperfection in this entire state of

being, in fact, was the niggling way her mind kept wanting to go back an hour and rehash everything Mark Stephanopolus had said to her in Lightyear Electronics. And everything she'd said to him. Had he flirted with her? Yes. Had she led him on? Um…no. Yes? Not intentionally. Not unless you counted her involuntary blushes and weak knees, but she couldn't be blamed for that.

Louis, who was seated just to her left and apparently feeling very entitled to her full attention because of how much time he'd spent this morning helping out her dad, chose that moment to hold up a pickle like a table microphone and address the assembled family. That included Lonnie, her mom and dad, sister-in-law Suzie, and sister Emma with boyfriend Jeff Bean. Alex wasn't there because he'd eaten earlier with Nick so the two of them could go to the outdoor skating rink at the town's rec center.

"I know there was a plan for us all to go out and see this housing development the Stephanopoluses are putting up…"

Ronnie gasped a little as she remembered, and understood why Mark had confidently asserted that *she'd* be coming to *him*.

Louis registered the gasp and obviously took it the wrong way as his voice took on a sour tone. "But as interesting as I'm sure that will be, I'm afraid that Ronnie and I are going to have to bow out."

Ronnie's mother clinked down the knife she'd been using to spread some mayonnaise on her sandwich bread, her whole face in distress. "Now why is that?"

"I like Mark and his father, but I did some research last night after dinner and realized that one of the clients I represent back in Chicago is in direct competition with Gold Construction, the Stephanopolus's company."

"Direct competition how?"

Louis waved a hand like it was nothing. "Just bidding on some project in a neighboring town."

"Lonsdon? Abbotsford?" Ronnie's mother pressed.

"Doesn't matter. Despite what I said last night, the whole region down here could indeed become a little hotspot of business development depending on how things go."

"Oh, I don't think so," said Ronnie's father. "In fact, I'm going to make sure it doesn't become a 'hot' spot ever. Slow, gradual growth."

Ronnie's mother turned to Ronnie. "Did you know your dad is running for city council this year?"

"About time!" Emma said from across the table.

"Congratulations," added Jeff quietly.

Suzie and Ronnie herself both chimed in with their own dittos and Ronnie started dinging her soup spoon on the edge of her bowl with a grin.

"Yes, congratulations!" Louis said, a loud enough to get everyone's attention. As they all turned to look at him, he smiled, "but the deals are still out there. They're still being negotiated. And Gold Construction is involved. Which means the problem of me being privy to confidential business practices or information still stands. Anything that Mark or his father, or even some worker at their building site, might let slip at this afternoon's outing is something I just do not want to accidentally overhear."

Ronnie's mother seemed to chew on Louis's rudeness for a moment, then on what he'd actually said, before her chin came up again. "All right. Then I guess you'll have to stay here. But I still want Ronnie to go."

Louis smiled and shook his head. "I'm afraid she can't go either."

"And why not?"

Ronnie herself frowned. "Yes. Why?"

Louis looked at her. "I really have to explain it to you?"

Ronnie's father, gaze darting back and forth between the talkers and obviously taken with the game now, said, "Please do."

"Apparently yes," said Ronnie in almost the same instant.

Louis turned his smile on her again. It was getting annoying. "Well, I was planning to keep this a surprise for Christmas morning. But I guess if it's that germane to this afternoon's plans, I'll have to jump the gun a bit."

Everyone waited, expectant but refusing to beg. Emma, actually, was at that moment distracted, wiping her boyfriend's chin where he'd just dribbled soup.

"The rules of confidentiality, as I'm sure Colin would tell you,"—he gave a nod of acknowledgement to Ronnie's father—"especially now if he's running for public office, can get pretty complicated and vary from situation to situation.

In this sort of business context, it's actually more a kind of conflict of interest or privacy of business knowledge that we're dealing with. And we could maybe argue that anything I saw or heard fit into a fuzzy exception to ethical practices." He made a wavy line in the air with his hand. "*But* I believe in keeping everything well within the best, most discrete of legal and business practices for my clients. For my law firm."

Ronnie's father leaned forward across the kitchen table at him and stabbed a forefinger at him. "Spit it out, boyo!"

"It's keeping the lines of communication clean. No accidental business information passed to me from Mark, from his father, from my wife to be."

Ronnie's mother gasped now, but it took a beat for Ronnie, who'd tuned out during Louis's long pontification about the rules of privilege or whatever, to soak in the last phrase.

She turned her whole body towards Louis. "What?"

His grin had grown even bigger. It looked to Ronnie like he meant to swallow her with it. "You heard me."

"Is that a proposal?" Ronnie said. The words seemed to be coming out of some part of her that was far away from where *she* was. Her elbow maybe. Her leg.

"A what?" cut in Emma from the end of the table, dragged back from where she'd been ostentatiously ignoring Louis's blather.

"That's a proposal," said Louis.

"No it's not!" said Emma, the fingers of her right hand still clenched tightly around the napkin she'd been using to wipe up Jeff's mouth. "A proposal, especially one to my sister, has to be done with some kind of…of…specialness."

Ronnie looked at Emma's unexpected defense of her and almost burst out crying.

"Like getting down on one knee," Jeff stuck in.

"Like that!" Emma said, dropping her napkin and grabbing Jeff's hand. Ronnie was glad Emma's gaze was still riveted on Louis and so couldn't see the tears welling up in her big sister's eyes.

Louis shrugged. "Like I said, it was supposed to be Christmas morning, but…" He pushed his chair back and stood. "You wait right here," he ordered Ronnie.

She couldn't have moved if her clothes were on fire. Her eyes were wet but her whole body had gone numb. Even just two weeks ago, she'd *expected* him to announce their engagement at any time. Certainly before Christmas. Because he knew, she'd even told him, that being able to announce an engagement over a Christmas dinner in her childhood home would be the single most perfect moment in her life to date.

But now?

He'd cheated on her, insulted her, coldly told her it was over. And true, he'd broken up with Vivienne, followed Ronnie up here through a snowstorm, sort of apologized, and she'd felt the old swell of emotions towards him, but…but she'd told him that he had to win her back. She'd made that clear. And here he was again just assuming she was his for the asking. His choice. His timing. His show.

But...*was* she his for the asking? Wasn't becoming his wife a key part of her life plan? And wasn't his whole he-who-hesitates-is-lost/take-no-prisoners approach to life part of what had attracted her to him in the first place?

And still she didn't move. Even through the long silence that fell around her like icicles that pinned her feet to the floor, her hands to the table, her bum to the seat of her chair. She sat still as she heard Louis run up the stairs, shuffle around up there, then thump his way back down. She barely twitched as he came back to her side, pulled his own chair out of the way, then physically turned her chair sideways to the table so that she faced him as he went down on one knee.

"Veronica Marilyn Cleary," he said as he smoothly pulled out a walnut-sized, red velvet box from his pocket and held it up dramatically between them, "would you do me the great honor..." He began to open the box so that Ronnie could just see a glint of a sparkle from the diamond band she knew was in there, that she'd so longed to see for so many months, when she'd been so sure that Louis was the perfect prince for her in every way, ready to guarantee her a place in the faster, bigger life of Chicago, permanently infuse her with his energy and upward trajectory, straighten out her unfocused, indecisive life...

"STOP!"

The voice that yelled it was so urgent, so commanding and hard, that Ronnie almost didn't recognize where it came from. Except the jerk in her chest and the shock on everyone else's face told her it had come from her.

And suddenly she was fully back in her body again, looking around her, taking in her mother's shock and worry, her sister's triumph, sister-in-law's surprise, her father's enigmatic calm, Jeff Bean's blinking, and Louis's...anger? Embarrassment? Both?

"Louis, if you'd planned to do it on Christmas, then I think it should wait at least until then. *Like we discussed.* Besides, if we're not even engaged, then I don't think your rules of privilege or exclusivity or inside knowledge or whatever it is can really apply to me, can it? Because I really want to go and see this development of the Stephanopoluses this afternoon. It sounds like fun." She looked at her watch, then at her mother. "So I think we'd better be going, right, Mom?"

Her mother, flustered, started fanning herself like she was having a hot flash. "Well, I don't know, dear... I mean..."

Ronnie's father pushed out his chair and stood brushing off his pants and grabbing bowl and plate from the table. "If we're going, let's be going."

Louis was glaring at her. "Ronnie..." he said in an undertone that was almost a growl. He was still down on one knee before her like he planned to block her from getting up. Ronnie felt her heart speed up as she realized that, for all her supposed feistiness, she'd rarely directly confronted Louis like this. Not on anything important. And never in front of a crowd of people.

Would he try to physically stop her? Order her to stay?

Insist on going himself so he could stick to her side like an unwelcome rash? She could just see how Mark would react to *that*.

And from yesterday believing that no man would ever want her, she suddenly seemed to have two men ready to lock horns and grunt and push at each other over her. That was almost worse.

Her rescue came from an unexpected source as Emma's Jeff got to his feet like Ronnie's dad and said, "I guess it's a matter of timing, isn't it. Ronnie obviously needs a bit of a breather before answering Louis's almost-question, and this afternoon outing gives her the chance. *I* think the outing sounds like fun, too. Hate to stay cooped up in the house all day when the sun's shining."

Emma was looking up at him a little agog. Even better, though, was the way Louis had to spin around to glare at him, thereby freeing Ronnie to pop quickly to her feet, scoop her plate and Louis's and their bowls, and hurry over to the kitchen sink. Then Emma was up and clearing. And Suzie and Ronnie's mom. And the momentum was all her way, the field trip underway. Louis's tense control of the moment was lost.

Ronnie avoided his eyes as he helped with the kitchen clean-up, and continued to do so when she went for her coat and gloves and boots, already otherwise dressed for an outing since she'd been out earlier.

Her heart was still going hard and she realized her face was flushed and hands clammy when she finally slipped out the door. Like she'd just avoided something horrible.

Louis's marriage proposal. She'd so yearned for it only a couple weeks ago and now it was horrible? Was that only because she didn't trust him anymore? Or didn't trust her own wanting of it? Or was it because of Mark? And if it was that last thing, was she completely insane?

6

So it's just down the road here a little," Mark said as he slapped his gloved hands together and stomped his booted feet.

Ronnie considered him as she waited for her mother and Emma to finish crawling out of the back of Alex's CR-V. Suzie had driven with Jeff riding up front with her. Ronnie and her dad had come in the pickup. They'd all decided that Alex and Nick weren't going to make it back from the skating rink in time, and that Nick wouldn't have been that interested anyway.

Mark stood in front of a Gold Construction pickup truck where he'd waved them to a stop in what looked like it would be a visitor's parking lot. She figured they were at the top of the hill leading down over the edge of Putter's Ridge, but it was hard to tell because, while Mayville was borderline prairie land, this stretch of hills had a beautiful stand of white pine like a scarf around the west end of town. It didn't stop the winter winds or snow, but it gave it a little more variety than the flatter lands to the south. And whatever kind of construction the Stephanopoluses were doing up here, they'd obviously been careful to keep as many of the evergreens as possible.

Cool. Very eco-friendly. Part of their environment.

Like Mark himself was, in this moment. Comfortable in jeans, he wore a flattering navy-blue fleece jacket and down vest. His gestures of being cold, Ronnie suspected, were strictly for the benefit of Jeff and Emma who hadn't dressed warmly enough. To empathize? Make them feel less silly for not attending to the Illinois cold?

It was hard to tell because Mark wasn't meeting Ronnie's eyes. In fact, despite the apparent consideration of Jeff and Emma, he looked...preoccupied. Like he was here because he'd promised he was going to show the Cleary clan the new development, but he wasn't really into it. Had something happened between this morning and now? Ronnie hated to admit it, but his sudden total lack of interest in her right now was disappointing.

"Um...exactly how far are we walking?" Emma asked from the back of the group.

And now Ronnie took the time to consider that too. It looked like the houses themselves had to be just down and to the left, looking out over the northwest end of town. But while the day-before's snowfall was plowed up in high banks all around the small parking area, the road to the construction site itself hadn't been touched, probably because the construction had been halted both for the snow storm and the Christmas holiday. Not good for Emma's short-boots-and-stretchy-leggings ensemble. Ronnie guessed that Jeff was a leg man and Emma, for all her put-on toughness, was still working hard to reel him in by displaying her best asset every chance she had.

Ha. Wouldn't look so good when they were frozen blue and white with frostbite.

Mark must have figured the same thing as he said, "Only forty or fifty yards down that trail and left. But it's pretty deep in places. Better have the people with good boots go first and tramp out a trail."

He finally turned to Ronnie and she was gratified to see his face visibly light up for a second, almost despite himself. Then he went serious again, as if he desperately wanted to talk to her about something, but obviously couldn't in this situation.

"Ronnie, you want to walk right behind me?" he said and held out a gloved hand to her.

She snorted but walked up to join him, ignoring the grins on both of her parents' faces. Ronnie *did* have good winter boots on that came up to mid-calf. And she'd tucked her jeans inside. Cinched the laces up tight around the top. It made her a regular Jungle Jane or Annie Oakley or something. Or just a daughter who knew what the winters in Mayville could be like and hadn't planned to be impressing a man anyway.

What was interesting, though, was how her insides had responded to Mark's serious look. Not a come-on or seduction. More like he really needed a friend. Inside Ronnie, she realized that she, too, could really use a friend right now. To talk to about Louis. And while Mark might have some obvious biases in that discussion, she somehow knew that he'd do his best to just listen first. And think it through without needing to comfort her like her father would do, or protect her like her brother and sister would do.

Mark leaned down to her ear as she joined him at the front of the troupe. "You look great," he said. A simple statement of fact.

"Same thing I was wearing when I saw you before lunch."

"You looked great then, too," he said. Again a serious statement of fact, when she was sure he'd normally accompany a statement like that with an eye twinkle. Or a grin. Something.

"You really want to talk about something, don't you," she gave back in the same even tone he'd given her.

He actually jerked his head back. Looked around, startled, as a couple snow-laden pine-tree branches beside them suddenly dumped their loads with a thump and swoosh. Then his eyes tracked Ronnie's mother and father and sister and boyfriend and sister-in-law.

"We better get moving," he said.

He turned and walked on ahead, stomping out a trail for her and the others with his boots. Ronnie followed.

And as they made their way down off the hilltop. For the first twenty yards or so, Ronnie concentrated on further flattening the trail Mark was cutting for them through the snow, both of them doing a kind of step-step-shuffle-about to make it easier for those who followed. Almost like a dance, Ronnie realized as she watched Mark's tight rear end sway and bump up and down before her and then almost copied his movements. *Whither thou goest, I will go...*

~~~~

Once he got past the insight of her comment and just walked, Mark found himself listening to Ronnie's stomping and shuffling behind him. It was a strange kind of syncopated dance they were doing that felt so natural he wanted to turn, take her in his arms and twirl her across the snow, then fall into it, wrapped together and laughing, everyone else back there be damned.

Except the others *were* there, of course. And he could hardly just let himself go right now even if they weren't. Not with this Stanco thing hanging over his head.

After getting off the phone with Stanco this morning, Mark had gone straight to his laptop, fired it up, and researched the heck out of Woodwand International, their business practices and philosophy. Then he'd gone back over all the research he'd done on Stanco itself, and admitted to himself that the company actually showed remarkable flexibility in their building practices. He'd verbally derided them as slash-and-burn developers last night at the Cleary dinner, but in fact there had been times when they'd gone very neighborhood-sensitive to build in a place that required it.

So if Mark could just draft guidelines that Stanco would have to follow, essentially making them tow Gold Construction's line, all he'd have to convince his father of was that the net benefits outweighed the risks. And that wouldn't be hard to do, given the Putter's Ridge numbers he'd been running with his father the day after he got home. Yes, GC *could* go it alone. But it was pretty extended. Until the entire project sold, GC was going to have a hard time moving on any other building opportunities at all. A big injection of cash and equipment would sure help.

Before Mark had had been able to put together a draft proposal, though, he'd had to come up here for this little family favor. A mini community show-and-tell. Which ironically was exactly the sort of thing Edward Stanco assumed he'd be doing more and more of—entertaining and selling development as the future to the residents of Middle America one family at a time.

Which also got Mark feeling conflicted again. Because when he touted the virtues of this development, however he did it, he was indirectly touting the buyout of their way of life, wasn't he? Well, maybe not the way of life of the younger generation, of Ronnie or her sister, but certainly of Colin and Evelyn Cleary, and of Mark's own parents.

Was that wrong, when the younger generation *wanted* the things that more development would provide? Was it?

Stomp, stomp. Shuffle, shuffle. Himself and Ronnie in almost a lock step.

And just like that he realized he'd been wrong, earlier, when he'd thought that any sort of feedback Ronnie would have to give him about Mayville's development would be interesting but ultimately too far off base to be useful. Instead, he had the sudden conviction that her perspective might be exactly what he needed. If nothing else, he sensed she would listen to him fairly without automatically judging him.

Or maybe she *would* judge him and that was what he needed.

But there was at least a sense that even if he were wrong about ending up with Ronnie, he could trust her to make this kind of discussion with her both confidential and filled with insight. Maybe it was the choices she'd made to go into confectionary work despite obvious pressures from her family. Maybe it was the way she held him off because she had a boyfriend and lived in Chicago, when other girls he'd had that physical vibe with had been ready to abandon everything else to be with him. Maybe it was that she'd looked into his eyes just a couple minutes ago and seen his need. Implicitly offered her services as listener.

Whatever it was, he realized he really did want her take on this.

Both for himself and for their future together.

As early as this afternoon, before the phone call from Stanco, he'd been planning a traditional courting press of painting her a picture of the two of them together, over and over. Basic advertising. You get a person imagining something often enough, voluntarily or not, and pretty soon they accept it as real.

Now his strategy, if he could call it that, was to just sit down somewhere and seriously *talk* with her. Figure himself out. Maybe figure her out a little bit in the process too. See if the two people they revealed themselves to be actually fit together.

Crazy.

Crazy and a little sad, is what his brothers would say.

And still he and Ronnie did their little dance—stomp, stomp, shuffle, shuffle. Making a path for the others, oh so symbolically.

Now if he could just figure out how to create a chance for a real conversation…

~~~~

Whither thou goest?

She was about to get angry about having such a subservient thought—in the Bible it wasn't even supposed to be about following a *man* at all; it was Ruth promising to follow her mother-in-law after her husband died—when they broke free of the pines and the sun-bright panorama of the town burst into sight before them, with its spread of glistening whiteness and shrunken houses and cars, little puffs of smoke from wood-burning fireplaces, and magical sense of distance. She felt the utter quiet but for the breath of wind through the trees behind them and a distant train whistle somewhere far off to the north.

"Oh my gosh," she heard Suzie breathe out just behind her.

"Wow," said Jeff, close behind Suzie.

They were the two people who hadn't grown up here, but even Ronnie, who vaguely remembered coming up here in the winter with her dad a few times when they were looking for good tobogganing hills, found herself sucking in such a sharp breath of the cold air that her lungs hurt. That God could make such beauty in the world…

She shook herself. Whoah. And she was thinking this shortly after that passage from the *Book of Ruth*. Had to be something about being back in a small Midwestern town for Christmas. It brought out the religion in her. Not her normal state of consciousness at all. Maybe triggered by Mark's thoughtful state? But still, the sheer beauty of it…

"The houses we're building are right down here," Mark said. "And we've got a little command office that's set up with electric heat and water if anyone gets desperate."

Ronnie lurched forward like she was coming out of a dream.

So they kept plowing on, with Mark and Ronnie doing their stomp-and-shuffle dance, until Mark had them stop beside a silent, snow-covered steam shovel and swivel to look downhill at one of an uneven row of large houses under construction. To the right of it was, as Mark had promised, a small, closed-in office of maybe ten-by-ten feet, that looked like it had been slapped together in a day with big squares of white siding and electric cables run in to give it heat.

Then everyone was there and Mark began giving a speech about the history and decisions that had gone into choosing the location, the construction techniques they'd had to develop to both shore up the hillside against erosion and protect the natural habitat around and throughout the project area.

But Ronnie only half-listened. In her opened-to-wonder state, she seemed to be able to see more than she normally would. It was almost like when she was coming up with a new candy recipe and could actually taste how it would turn out. Or, going back further, how she'd see a company's product or a head office or staff and see immediately how they could all come together in a set of beautiful, linked web pages. Here and now she could see the homes going up, how they would catch the morning sunrise from the east, the dew melting from the grass as the sun climbed higher. She could hear cars roaring out of their garages and roaring back later. And car doors opening and thunking shut again as little...kids...ran out of the garage and up the hills to the forest, while their parents, smiling, carried baseball gear into the house.

"Ronnie?"

"Hm?" She turned to find her father standing at her shoulder, nudging her. She looked at him, then followed his chin point and saw Mark watching her. "What?"

"I asked if you could see yourself moving into a place like this," Mark said.

"Here? Gorgeous, but not a chance."

He looked deeply interested. "Why?"

She shrugged to cover the sudden shortness of breath high in her chest. "My life's in Chicago. I love the city. I love my life there. That's all."

Mark narrowed his eyes and nodded. "Okay."

"What do you mean, 'Okay'?"

"I just mean okay. Some people want to live in small towns and have them never change. Some want to live there and help them grow. Some want to get out completely and go to places that are already grown. Like Chicago."

Despite the biting cold, Ronnie felt her face burn. "You know I spend enough time justifying my life to my parents." She looked back at them. "Sorry, Mom. Dad." She whipped her gaze back to Mark. "I don't have to justify it to you."

"Of course you don't have to justify it to me," Mark said, surprised. "I was only— Forget it." He turned away from her to look at the rest of the project, as if trying to figure out what more he had to show them.

Ronnie's dad stepped up beside her, supporting her arm like he was worried she was going to fall. He waved his hand along the other roughed-in houses. Hard to tell through all the trees that had been left standing, but there looked to be twelve of them. They'd all had their concrete foundations poured, but only this first one that Mark had stopped them in front of had been almost finished.

"You going to show us the others?" Ronnie's dad asked.

"Not really much to see," Mark said, carefully not looking at Ronnie.

Like his earlier desire to talk to her had been replaced by a desperate desire to just get away from her, to see the last of her. She was the too-spicy woman again. Sure Louis could come back for her, but... Wait, why *had* Louis come back for her?

"The foundations," Ronnie's father said. "The floor plans. Your father's never taken me through one of his building sites before."

"Sure. Your wish is my command, Mr. Cleary. But no one's allowed to fall into an open foundation and sue, okay? Stay close. There are some slippery parts."

He directed the last comments mostly to Jeff and to Ronnie's mother, apparently having decided, through observation, that the others, including Emma and her ankle boots, were actually pretty sure footed. Jeff, sweetie that he was, offered his arm to Ronnie's mother. It probably earned him brownie points with Emma, but Ronnie figured it also quadrupled the chances of both of them falling, now that either one could drag the other down.

Ronnie was reassured when she saw her father step back to follow close behind the two of them, so Ronnie herself fell into her usual spot just behind Mark, stomping out a path for the others as they went.

Then it happened.

The others fell a little behind because they stopped to peer into an open foundation. Mark saw it and stopped dead. Not running away from her at all. In fact, when he looked at her now, it was with such a sudden fierceness that Ronnie found herself actually taking half a step backwards.

"Look," he said. "I know this sounds crazy because you hardly know me, but I really need to talk with you."

Ronnie swallowed, feeling an involuntary rush of heat that ran right to her sex. "About what?"

"About…" He paused, clearly wanting to speak and just as clearly not sure if he should.

"If this is about you and me, or me and Louis…"

"No. Not about that."

"Not?"

"I mean, that's on my brain as well and I figure it will come up at some point. Has to. But no, that's not it."

"Then what?" She realized she must have a really one-track brain, thinking that whatever Mark Stephanopolus had to say would have had to be about her. Heaven knew that everything *she* really wanted to talk about with him was about her. Egocentric much, Ronnie?

He looked deep into her eyes, as if searching for something, and seemed to find it. "It's this project," he said.

"What do you—? You mean this building project? The houses?"

"Yes, you know that Gold Construction's only sold six of these houses so far, right?"

"That's what my mother said. And I can't say I'm surprised. I checked out Gold Construction's website. Seriously not helping. And no social networking that I could see. Facebook? Twitter?"

"But I think we'll still sell the rest of them by May. So when I graduate…"

Good grief. *This* was what this was about? Selling her on how successful he was going to be here. "When you graduate," she snapped, "you'll be back here supervising the building, getting ready to take over the company, right?"

"Yes, but…"

"You won't?"

"I will."

"And I'll be back in Chicago. Maybe getting married to Louis."

He frowned and looked down at his fur-lined construction boots like this was not at all what he'd been trying to talk about. And instantly Ronnie felt foolish. She'd made it all about her again. She lifted her chin and cleared her throat.

"Sorry. I was jumping to conclusions again. It sounded like you were selling me on life here in Mayville after I told you I'm not leaving Chicago. Like you were a greedy little kid who was saying 'Look at me! Look at me! This is the life you want!'"

One corner of his mouth quirked up. "You think I'm a greedy little kid?"

"Well you did start talking all about you. I was assuming that's because you're used to putting your own needs and desires first."

Something almost like shame flashed over his face. Followed by a rueful smile. "You really think I'm that egocentric?"

"I'm… I told you I'm not leaving Chicago, so why do you even bother talking to me?"

"Maybe because of that. I told my own father that I'd never leave Boston. Unless it was maybe to move to New York."

She stared at him. "Really?"

"Really." Now he looked east over the little town of Mayville like he could see far past it, all the way to Massachusetts. "I actually started looking for intern positions in Boston the day I started my fall term last September. I figured I'd take almost anything, live cheaply, learn the ropes of a business, any business, and start building a life on the east coast. Or any big city, really. Be where the action is. And I got a good offer."

Ronnie frowned. "Then why come back here?"

"It's complicated. My dad had a series of small heart attacks last year. He won't tell me, but my mom hinted at it and his doctor confirmed it. Basically, if he keeps up the stressful pace he's had running his business these last eighteen months without me, he's going to have another one and die. I'm not going to let that happen."

Ronnie thought of her own father and had to fight back a lump in her throat. "Wow. Just…wow. So you really are a

George Bailey. Trapped by the demands of family."

"That's how you see it? Being trapped by family? Is that why you're so determined to stay in Chicago?"

"I've always hated that movie."

Mark smiled sheepishly. "You know, I actually did too. Once upon a time. It's probably why I picked Harvard for my MBA. Because it was a long way away from here."

"Sure, that's why anyone picks Harvard. Just like that."

"A long way both in distance and in…life outlook?"

"Right. Of course." Ronnie blushed and looked down at her own boots. "But then your dad has a heart attack. And despite having two older brothers, it's you who has to come flying back."

"Neither of them knows construction. Besides, it wasn't just my father…"

"Then what? The pretty views?"

His face had gone dead serious again, like he was about to reveal something important, but before he could answer, the rest of the group had obviously had their little look-see and caught up to them, ending the conversation. Mark swept his features clear and turned from her to face them all.

"So. Twelve houses. Each one's a different design and each one's almost infinitely customizable, so long as the owners keep things in character with the general aesthetic of the development. If the first set sells out, we have dibs on developing another couple acres of the ridge."

"It's outside of town," Suzie piped up. "I thought you said

your dad's company tries to build in existing neighborhoods."

"It's only about ten minutes once the road up's properly finished," Mark said, "but yes, there's a bit of guesswork in this case. Word is…" He put his fingers to his lips like he was sharing a secret.

~~~~

What was he doing? Why? Because he'd been about to tell Ronnie and been interrupted? *Confession interruptus.* Good grief.

He obviously couldn't spill everything Stanco Bros. was planning. Of course not. That would have been a breach of the implicit agreement he had with them. But the most recent thing Edward had told him—about this other company entering the picture—hadn't been part of that. Wasn't even solid in fact. He'd presented it as a possibility. And if Mark, too, presented it now as a possibility? What would that gain him? Maybe impress them with his business knowledge, which would actually help along the Stanco plan of him garnering their trust and goodwill. Maybe it could also be a trial balloon that he floated by them all to see their reaction. Ronnie's reaction, in particular.

So he cleared his throat, leaned forward, and said with a stage whisper. "The word is that Woodwand International might move its head production facility near this end of town in the new year. Meaning more people, more business, more money." He gestured at the twelve homes begun. "All of these snapped up with the Phase Two development guaranteed."

He straightened up and waited. Ronnie's father had knit his brows so deeply that the eyebrows actually touched. Okay. Not surprising, giving his anti-development comment at the table last night. It was more the reaction of the others he was interested in. Was Edward Stanco right about the Midwest being full of people sticking their heads in the dirt and fighting progress with their free hands and feet?

Ronnie's mother spoke first. "Woodwand. They do furniture, don't they?"

"Yes they do," said Mark. "Conservative. Known for quality work. Ranked as a top one hundred employer for the way they emphasize quality of life issues for their employees and zero-emissions for their factories. Which is why, when they move to a place, they usually keep their presence low profile."

Jeff piped up, "Hey, maybe *I* should go and work for them!"

Everyone chuckled but Mark, who said, "Laugh, but it's the way of the future. Pardon my attack on the legal profession, Mr. Cleary, but I had a lot of friends in school who went into law and are now killing themselves in big firms. I can't help but think the trend in the next couple decades is going to be finding more sustainable lifestyles."

"Like moving to a small town," Ronnie's dad said with a nod, looking directly at Ronnie.

Okay. Interesting. Ronnie wouldn't like the pressure, but if she saw that Mark was part of something her father approved of, it couldn't be the work of the devil, right?

"Of course, assuming I'm elected to Town Council in a couple weeks," Ronnie's father continued, "I'll be demanding we see exactly what their long-term plan is and what guarantees they provide. What happens too often with these things is they become the thin edge of the wedge. First a nice development like this makes the town look attractive, but still homey. Then a big business moves in, the town grows to accommodate it, it catches the eyes of a bigger business. Pretty soon the small-town hominess that attracted everyone here has vanished in the flood of quick townhouses and strip malls."

He looked directly at Mark and held his gaze in the way Mark imagined he had used when cross-examining witnesses in a courtroom. "I know that's not your intention, Mark. Heaven knows that your father's company has done more to make this town beautiful than a host of flower planting by-laws. And I've no doubt you'll honor his building ethic. Just saying that I've seen an influx of business work well, and I've seen it change a town for the worse. Eco-friendly or not."

Mark just stared. He finally managed to close his open mouth before he asked about the only part of the speech that truly sank in…and possibly changed everything about this game.

"You're running for town council?"

7

LATER THAT NIGHT, as Ronnie helped Alex stoke the fire in the living room for the traditional Cleary Christmas Eve, she found herself running over and over Mark's reaction to her father's anti-development speech out at the building site. Especially the way Mark, his face looking vaguely pale, had asked whether Colin Cleary was running for town council.

No one else seemed to have noticed Mark's pallor or his hesitation in answering further questions that Ronnie's dad had put to him. And that scared Ronnie too.

Not so much because it signaled that whatever he'd been about to tell her earlier was probably something her father wouldn't approve of. Maybe even something illegal or...what? Something about the Gold Construction project that made Mark ashamed or at least concerned.

No, what concerned her was, first, that she'd been the only one to see the change in his expression, which meant that she'd become far too attentive to those facial expressions, his deep and thoughtful eyes, every twitch of his lips. This should not be. Her life plan had her working and living in Chicago. Probably married to Louis. The last thing she needed was getting physical infatuated with Mayville's reluctant favorite son.

And even more concerning was that, second, even if that guy, Mark Stephanopolus, was doing something he shouldn't that might hurt Ronnie's father, Ronnie wasn't going to blow his cover.

Because…because…she somehow knew Mark trusted her not to and *she*, foolishly, wanted to honor that trust. More than that, even. She actually believed that if he was doing something he thought her father might not approve of, it was probably for a good reason. The man had given up his career dreams to look after his ailing father, for Pete's sake!

And what had Ronnie done like that? What had Ronnie ever done to honor her parents or prove herself worthy? Make candies? Invent a new type of peanut brittle? Good grief, maybe Louis *was* right that she was still just splashing about in the kiddy pool of life. She couldn't figure out her career. She couldn't stop looking at handsome guys. Guy. Singular. Whom she also admired and was getting not a little fascinated by. Which was *stupid!*

A hand grabbed her wrist and she almost dropped the poker. Baby brother Alex.

"Hey!" she said.

"I think it's poked," he said calmly and directed her gaze to the fire.

The half-burned log she'd attacked looked like someone had been trying to chop it with an axe. It was gouged and cracked and so far back in the fire box it looked ready to lie there and die all by its lonesome.

"I guess," she said.

"Shall we add another log to make up for it?" Alex had already picked up a split log from the tin wood-basket nearby and handed it to her. He watched as she delicately placed it on top of the main stack, where it seemed to catch almost immediately, hissing and popping as its air pockets superheated.

"So, Sis, how *was* the trip up to see Mark's building project?"

"You mean his dad's project." It came out sharper than she'd intended and she stared into the fire to hide her discomfort. Behind her, through the door to the kitchen, the rest of the family was gathered, visiting and making a big salad together while Ronnie's mom got the traditional tortiere meat pies into the oven. That meant they'd be eating within the hour. Then there would be some Christmas carols sung around the piano, with Ronnie's mom playing. Then it was off to midnight mass and a late bedtime. Particularly for Alex and Suzy who had to lay out a Christmas stocking and "present from Santa" for Nick after he was in bed.

"Sure," Alex said. "His dad's project. Which he's going to be running come springtime. Something bad happen while you were out there? Or something good?"

Ronnie looked sharply at him. She might be the only one who could read Mark Stephanopolus, but apparently she herself was much easier to read. At least by her baby brother, who'd inherited his dad's genes and stood almost a foot taller than Ronnie.

"Nothing happened," Ronnie said.

"Because I heard about Louis's, you know, proposal thing. If you don't mind me saying, I'm not sure you two are such a great fit."

"Wha—? Louis wasn't even at the tour of the building project."

"I know. But Mark was doing the tour, right? Mom said you and he walked and talked a lot, separate from everyone else. And you don't have to say anything about it. I just want you to know that I've bumped into Mark a few times, played some pickup hockey with him. He's a good guy. Always fair. Always thinking of others, you know?"

"*So?*" There it was again. The small-town values thing that Ronnie had thought she might inject a little of into Louis. And the fact that Mark already had it didn't help because he *was staying in a small town!*

Alex shrugged. "Nothing. Just putting that out there."

Ronnie shook her head. "I don't believe this. I do not believe this." She turned from him and stomped into the kitchen so she could GO AND HAVE A GOOD TIME. And deal with Louis Beauchamps. Become a grown up and put Mark Stephanopolus out of her mind for good.

~~~~

At the same time, Mark and his family clan of sixteen (because his mother's sister and family had joined the immediate Stephanopolus thirteen) were heading out to the same Catholic church that the Clearys would be going into for midnight mass in a few hours. They'd had their traditional egg-lemon chicken-and-rice soup and the women had gotten a start on the Christopsomo (bread of Christ) loaf for tomorrow, as well as prep for the stuffed cabbage, pork, and tons of sweats, most of which had been off the menu for the last forty days leading up to Christmas.

Mark had offered to help, and, as usual, had been shoved out of the kitchen. He'd gone back to his room to polish his proposal that he planned to discuss with his father the day after Christmas, but his brothers had found him there and dragged him with them to check out the skating rink that an old high-school friend of Stephano's had made on his property. They'd gone to the local rink with their skates and hockey sticks when Mark had been doing his Putter's Ridge thing and found it too crowded. So Aaron had gotten Stephano to text his friend, Stony, and see if he'd done one this year. And he had. Why didn't they come and check it out? If they liked it, he was organizing a hockey game for Christmas day with a few other people he knew. The more, the merrier.

Now, walking to church with his burly brothers and workman father all stuffed into collared shirts and ties under their parkas, Mark smiled to himself as he remembered them all putting on their skates and ripping around on Stony's private rink. His own private skating rink! How perfect was that? Everything about this town was so many worlds removed from Harvard and the big city business moves and hustles. Right now especially. It was peaceful, chilly, and a little surreal with the full moon rising up in a mostly clear night sky. But it was...good.

Which of course was what Colin Cleary was trying to preserve in his run for Mayville's town council, what Mark's own father believed in, and what Edward Stanco wouldn't understand if you hit him upside the head with a Christmas wreath made with fresh pine branches cut from a white pine tree up on Putter's Ridge.

So what was Mark doing in bed with the bad guys? Well, maybe facing reality? Living with the inevitable that his father and Ronnie's father both refused to prepare for. Mark would do his best to make sure Stanco *did* honor Mayville's small-town feel, but the crowded skating rink his brothers told him about was just one sign of the simple fact that towns always changed. Usually they grew or they died.

And if growth changed his home too much? Mark mentally shrugged. It wasn't really his home if he couldn't live here, was it? And he could never live here long-term if the girl he found himself irresistibly drawn to didn't want to live here either. *My life is in Chicago*, Ronnie had said. Not here. Despite the way she looked in a winter parka and proper snow boots, stomping through knee-high snow like this landscape had been made just for her.

Mark shook his head.

Was he really thinking that? Considering giving up everything he had here or in Boston to follow a girl to Chicago? After working through this thing with his father and the Stancos, of course, but... Wow. This Christmas was shaping up to be crazy in so many ways.

He looked up and picked out the brightest star he could see and wondered if there was a census being taken right now in the land of Illinois to identify the true sons and daughters of the land so that the first-borns, or the true believers, could all be killed off by King Heedless Progress before they could become a threat.

"Unless here in this small town, this night," he whispered to himself, "is born a small child inside me, in Ronnie, in our fathers, who will rise up and lead our people to a better way of life."

"You say something, Marky?" said big brother Aaron, who was just a step behind him and half-wrestling with his son Benjy as they walked.

Mark blew out a steamy breath, laughed, and shook his head. "Just imagining miracles," he said.

"Like you and the Cleary chick hooking up?"

"Say what?"

"Mom mentioned you two kind of hit it off on that dinner thing a couple nights ago."

"You mean before her boyfriend from Chicago showed up to spend Christmas with them?"

He tried to make it come out light, but Aaron clapped an arm around his shoulders, something only he and Chris, Mark's other older brother, had ever been comfortable doing with Mark. Because Mark intimidated people, he knew, with his combination of broad shoulders and serious mind. They'd never been quite able to figure him out. Even in high school, the girls had fawned, the coaches for the various sports teams had tried to draft him, and he'd mostly ignored them all. He'd usually been too busy getting good grades and learning the family business at Gold Construction during his spare time.

Yeah, and look where that had gotten him.

But his big brothers, who were at least as burly as Mark, had sat on him and wrestled with him since he was barely a year old, so they had no reservations about grabbing him however and whenever.

Now Aaron leaned his head in close to Mark's as they walked and spoke low. "You know, when I met Tiffany, she thought I was a Grade A jackass."

"I heard that!" called out his son Benjy and Chris's son, Brent, who'd looked, up to a second ago, like they were totally immersed in a thumb-wrestling match as they walked.

"So did everyone else, sweetie!" called up Tiffany, still a dynamic little woman in her bouncy-haired, full-figured way. "But everyone remembers it anyway, so that's alright!"

"But I kept right on chasing her…," said Aaron.

"He was a real pain in the rear," Tiffany said.

"…until she finally gave in and went out with me."

"To dinner at MacDonald's!" shouted the boy cousins in unison. It was a familiar story.

"So if you need to win this babe..."

"What?" Mark asked. "Invite her out to MacDonald's?"

"No, doof-head!" Aaron let go of his shoulders and ground his knuckles into Mark's head. "You keep bugging her! Weren't you listening?"

"Yeah, *doof*-head!" screamed the cousins and broke into their eleven and twelve-year-old giggles.

At which point Mark's mother finally deemed it wise to turn back from where she led the procession of family. Her glare quieted everyone down, even the boys, as they approached the front steps of Saint Joseph's and joined the back of the crowd funneling down and in through the front doors.

Mark did a quick check around to see if he could spot Ronnie, but couldn't. He suspected the Clearys went to midnight mass. They seemed pretty traditional Catholics from some of the comments they'd made last night over dinner. But this was one tradition he didn't envy them. The idea of trying to get Benjy and Brent, or worse, Stephano's littler ones, Justin and Sherry, to stay up late enough to go and sit still for a church service at their ages was just laughable.

No, better to have an early evening service, come home and hang the small presents for New Year's Eve on the tree, then get everyone to bed early so they could all start the day right with lots of food, presents, and, thanks to Stephano's texting earlier, *hockey!* Put the whole Stanco business out of his mind for at least Christmas day.

Mark paused for just a moment outside the door leading into the church and looked up again at the moon and stars. He breathed in the cold night air and wished he could also, for that one magic day, spend some time just being with Ronnie.

He closed his eyes, knowing that she'd no doubt be totally taken up with Cleary traditions, just as he'd be taken up with Stephanopolus ones.

And the one chance they might have to get to know each other without Edward Stanco's threats coming between them would be gone, and all he'd have left to offer her would be either his successful-but-compromised self, or his virtuous-but-career-going-bye-bye self.

Yes, they'd be part of each other's life somehow. He still believed it. But if he had a Christmas wish, it would be this—to meet her again for at least one day of simple fun and enjoyment before all the tough stuff came down.

Just that, he breathed, then opened his eyes again and entered the church.

8

RONNIE SLEPT THAT NIGHT and dreamt of living, smooth-wood furniture. The table and chest of drawer and chairs and coat-rack thing were dressed in Santa hats and danced around the Cleary house while Mark gaily conducted their music with a long pointy black baton.

Christmas morning she woke up feeling disoriented. Then she saw Louis sleeping on the carpet with his sheet and blankets balled up around his neck, half-strangling him where he slept, and remembered everything. She gave a little moan, slipped out of bed, into her robe, and crept out the door. It was Christmas. It was *Christmas!* For one day, at least, she could put all her self-doubts and Movie-of-the-Week dilemmas on hold.

She stopped in the bathroom only briefly, then joined her mother, father, and sister in the kitchen. A steaming cup of eggnog-flavored latte and some Christmas-morning muffins brought her to a warm and happy place, absorbing the homey talk of the early risers and listening to Nick tear through his Christmas stocking. Forty minutes or so after that, with the whole house awake and gathered in the living room, Ronnie's dad read the little tags on each gift under the Christmas tree and handed them out one at a time.

There were books and e-readers and sweaters and jewelry and power tools (for Jeff from Emma! Ha!) and perfume (Louis to her; she'd warned him ahead of time to hold onto his ring until at least New Year's like they'd agreed) and car doodads and so much more that by the end of it she felt guilty over the abundance of material wealth, but even richer in the sense of family surrounding her. No, she couldn't really ever go home again—she'd been so ready to leave when she headed off for university—but if you were lucky, you could maybe step back in for a deep bath of love. Chester had been so right on that score.

Even so, after she'd helped her mom and siblings clear up the wrapping paper and plastic and clean the kitchen, she gasped in delight at Alex's suggestion that the second and third generations all head out to a private rink he'd been invited to yesterday for a little shinny hockey like they'd done as kids. Space to move! Fresh cold air! Yes!

Ronnie and Suzie both had to scrounge through the basement storage locker to come up with some usable ice skates, and Suzie's fit acceptably only after she'd put on four pairs of socks, but hey. With a clash and clatter of skates and hockey sticks and pucks, plus buckets for goal posts, they were out the door.

Louis drove her and Emma and Jeff in the Land Rover.

Alex led the way in his CR-V with Suzie and Nick. Ronnie's mom and dad had decided to sit this one out back at home.

They drove to the north end of town, almost like they were heading back up to Putter's Ridge, but turned off the highway to head toward Rolston, then right again, into what looked like a private dairy farm. Ronnie saw a decent two-story house in white clapboard with green trim dead ahead, but the drive split left and right ahead of it, the left track veering down through a windbreak of pine and coatrack poplar. That was the track they took.

It led to an open yard dotted with a bullet-shaped water tower, a series of sheds and two large barns that were puffing and grunting out steam or exhaust from their long, low-pitched roofs. Cold day. That was probably where the animals were kept.

Ronnie's group didn't get as far as the barns, however. Alex parked them just past the water tower and gestured for everyone to get out.

Ronnie did, grabbed her skates and hockey stick, and jogged over to him, puffing great clouds of steam into the air as she did. The hard-packed-and-sanded ground under her feet crunched and squeaked as the others joined them. The air smelled sharp and cold, with just a faint aftertaste of cow dung.

"Stony Phelps," Alex said as he opened the rear of his SUV and sat Nick up on the edge of it to help him tighten up the skates he'd obviously put on in the car. Alex looked over his shoulder at Ronnie as he worked. "You remember him from high school? This is his folks' place, but he pretty much runs it now. Ran into him at the public rink in town yesterday and we got talking. Turns out he made a rink for his daughters, who are both in figure skating. But Stony misses playing hockey and has been trying to rustle up enough people for a game. Said the rink's just past the equipment shed here. He's shoveled a path."

"Pretty cool," Ronnie said, then noticed for the first time that Louis hadn't brought along skates. "Oh my goodness, Louis! I never even checked to see if you had any skates. You seemed so enthusiastic…"

He smiled, shrugged with uncharacteristic humility, and held up a fancy-looking camera she hadn't noticed him arriving with. "Borrowed this from your dad. Decided I'd be the official photographer and videographer. Save the Christmas morning memories."

Ronnie walked over to him and looked up into his face with a surge of tenderness. "Thank you, Louis. That's really sweet of you."

He grinned down at her. "Can't guarantee many pictures of anyone other than you, mind you. But I'll try." Then he leaned down close to her ear so only she could hear, and added, "I am trying, Ronnie."

She nodded and gave his arm a quick squeeze.

"Is it just us?" Emma asked, looking around at their small group.

"Nah," said Alex, straightening up to let Nick hop down now, skates tied tight. "Stony's got his wife, his girls, who are just a couple years older than Nick, and another few guys who happened to text him yesterday while we were talking. They were at the same rec center rink we were at and didn't know it. I looked through the crowd and saw them. Cracked me up."

"Anyone we know?" asked Ronnie.

"Oh, I think so," he said casually. "One of them, at least."

Then he ducked his head and hurried to the path past the equipment shed in a way that made Ronnie suddenly very wary as she took Louis by the hand and followed him.

~~~~

"Score!" yelled Mark's baby brother, Stephano, and pumped his fist as he glided around the back of their bucket goal posts.

Little twerp, Mark grinned. Gets old enough to score a hot wife and have two cute kids and suddenly thinks he's a hockey god. And Stony and Chris were encouraging him, cheering like a couple of madmen.

While they celebrated, Mark skated hard to the back of the rink to dig the puck out of the snow and came charging back towards Stephano's end with it, deftly executing a give-and-go with Aaron's son, Benjy, to get around Chris and his son, before whipping it neatly between the bucket and work boot they'd set up as goal posts on *that* end.

As he circled the goal posts with a cocky grin and high-fived his eleven-year-old nephew for his assist, he saw a new batch of players had arrived. Then almost tripped over his own skates as he took in who they were.

His prayer last night. He hadn't even been inside the church when he'd made it, but it had been granted anyway, without him even having to get obnoxious about it and drum up some sort of excuse to casually drive over to Duck Lane where the Cleary family lived.

Skating casually to the side of the rink where Stony had set up some carpets and a half-dozen lawn chairs on a shoveled-out seating area just over the built-up edge of the rink, Mark raised his stick in greeting to Alex Cleary, the youngest of the sibs but the one he'd actually played hockey with before. He had his son with him, as he had had at the community skating rink, though now Mark barely recognized the kid because Alex had found an old hockey helmet from somewhere and plopped it on his son's head.

Alex gave him a grin, raised his own stick, and called, "Well look who's here! Can't get rid of you, I guess."

Stephano's and Aaron's wives were still over near the snow-covered, old, junked farm equipment with Stephano's little ones and Stony's girls, but suddenly Aaron and Chris, their sons, and Stephano were all up beside Mark like an official greeting party.

As Mark turned to finally greet Ronnie, his heart dipped a little to see Louis at her right arm. They looked every inch a couple as they approached the rink and Ronnie commandeered one of the lawn chairs to put on her skates. She hadn't met Mark's gaze.

Louis, Mark noted, was carrying a camera, not skates. That was promising.

A few minutes of skate tying and introductions later, the two teams squared off. Alex had insisted Ronnie join him against Mark and whomever. Which meant that Mark and Chris stayed teamed up, along with Chris's son, Brent; Ronnie's sister, Emma; and Emma's boyfriend, Jeff. Aaron and his son kept Stony and Stephano, and added Ronnie, Alex, and Alex's wife, Suzie. It looked a little lopsided towards Aaron's team, but actually Chris could skate rings around everyone on the ice and his son, though only eleven, had inherited his dad's hockey gifts.

And with this many newbies, it was going to be a friendly match anyway. Stony laid out the rules. No body checks. No serious scorekeeping. Mark and his brothers were so fiercely competitive amongst themselves that Mark worried their earlier play might have scared Stony a little, but they knew how to tone it down.

Mostly.

Actually, Mark thought as he tried hard to keep a goofy grin off his face, the only thing he didn't like was the fact they weren't allowed to do body checks. It would have been so easy to casually tumble Ronnie into the snow bank and fall on top of her.

As it was, he was so distracted by her presence on the ice, constantly aware of the flash of red hair coming loose from her snow hat, of the determined, graceful way she moved in her form-fitting jeans and puffy green bomber jacket, that Aaron slipped a puck right around him before Mark even realized the game had begun. Chris poke-checked him to take the puck away, but when he passed it Mark's way, it sailed right by for Stephano to scoop up.

"Uncle Mark!" Brent screamed. "Jeez!"

"Brent!" Chris snapped.

"But Dad…"

The kid was skating backwards in a fancy S-curve to block his more with-it uncle Stephano, who finally had to pass back to Stony, who passed to Suzie, who bumped it over to Alex, who deftly skated around Emma and scored.

"Argh!" Brent again.

"Friendly game, son," said Chris, skating by the boy and scrubbing his head with a gloved hand. "Keep repeating that to yourself. And *you*," he said and pointed at Mark, "start playing a little maybe?"

"Yessir!" Mark said and saluted.

But even when Mark tried to get his head back into the game, his crafty younger brother just gently sailed the puck over to Ronnie, who skated hard towards Mark like a pro… except she kept her head mostly down, watching the puck on her stick. Mark would have normally skated backwards and used his stick to easily scoop it away from her, but all he could do was stare.

The inevitable collision that followed, tumbled them both off their skates. Mark grabbed her as they went down to make sure she fell on top of him and didn't hurt herself. Which unfortunately meant his own right elbow hit first, then his tailbone and right shoulder as he curled his head up hard to avoid a concussion. It felt like a giant had grabbed him by the feet and thwacked him down hard on cement. Pain earthquaked through the right side of his body and he buried his face into the back of Ronnie's jacket to hide his involuntary grimace and tears.

"Whoah!" he heard Aaron cry from somewhere. "Time! Penalty shot! I mean…you okay, bro?"

Then he and Chris and Stony were pulling Ronnie up off him. She seemed to be fine, muttering, "I'm okay, okay? Just… clumsy." Which wasn't true. *Mark* had been the clumsy one. Distracted and clumsy. Great way to make an impression. Even better, just lying there on the ice, hardly able to move. It took all his willpower not to groan or swear.

Then Stephano was down on his knees beside him. "Mark, you okay? Anything broken?"

He shook his head. Realized he tasted blood in his mouth. Must have bitten his tongue. "Only thing broken is my dignity. Give me a hand?" Then he did groan as Stephano pulled him up and he limp-skated over to the lawn chairs. "Gonna sit out for a bit," he managed.

Stephano nodded and went back to the others. Louis,

Mark noted, had left his standing position behind the lawn chairs when Mark had limped over, and now stood in his city boots on center ice where Ronnie was surrounded by her sister and sister-in-law, who seemed to be checking her out head to toe like some kind of NHL on-ice docs.

Mark grimaced and closed his eyes. Aw, poor baby. Maybe now Louis would escort her off and convince her that hockey was a stupidly dangerous sport and they should instead just go driving around town in his borrowed Range Rover for fun.

But when he opened his eyes, he saw Ronnie looking his way and apparently arguing with Louis and her sisters. A moment later she was skating over to his side of the rink, Louis following slowly in a slippery-boot shuffle. Ronnie stepped over the edge of the rink, walked two more steps, plopped down into the lawn chair immediately to his left, and blew out.

"Stupid sport," she said.

"Best sport in the world," Mark said.

"That's what I meant."

"When you're actually playing it and not distracted watching the beautiful players on the other—" He cut himself off as Louis finally reached them in a mad running-backwards-in-place slowdown motion that had him windmilling his arms for balance, his expensive-looking camera swinging wildly on its neck strap.

When Louis had regained his balance and stepped off the ice onto the less-slippery crunch of the snow and carpets, he beat his gloved hands together, blew out a cloud of steam, and grinned at Mark, showing his teeth. "Guess I should thank you for saving my fiancée from a bad fall out there, hunh?"

Out of the corner of his eye, Mark saw Ronnie flush red. "Fiancée?" he said.

"He asked," Ronnie said. "I haven't answered yet."

"Very true. Very true," Louis said. "There's always the chance that she'd rather settle down here in Mayville with a local boy, I suppose. Become a housewife and work at the local coffee shop or something. You think she'd enjoy that, Mark? It is Mark, right? College boy who's coming back to Mayville to take over his father's building company?"

"More or less," Mark said. He could actually see a spot of crimson in Ronnie's face that made her hair look pale. And that was saying something.

"Hey!" Louis said. "I'm talking to you here!" He leaned forward and waved a hand in front of Mark's face.

Mark blinked and turned his head to look back at Louis. With Ronnie right there, not to mention his sorely aching body right now, the last thing he was inclined to do was take offence at someone obviously too stupid to live. Or maybe Louis sensed all that. Maybe he'd read the situation and decided that this situation was actually the perfect time to call Mark out and finish the pseudo-intellectual thrashing he'd intended to administer a couple nights back.

"You're not seriously going to do this, are you?" Mark said quietly.

Louis's grin was almost a snarl. "If you mean am I going to tell you to keep your small-town mug away from the woman I'm going to marry, then yes. That's exactly what I'm doing."

"You know I'm right here," Ronnie said to Mark's left.

"What she said," Mark said, his gaze having not left Louis's. "But it really has nothing to do with her, does it Louis. It is 'Louis' isn't it? As in pompous lawyer clown who thinks he's only on top if he manages to put down everyone around him who might be a threat."

"Mark…"

Ronnie's tone should have made him stop right there, but somehow, just in the way Louis had grinned at him and assumed he could push Mark around, he'd essentially turned into Edward Stanco, and the obnoxious students he'd had to compete with this last term at Harvard, and even, somehow, every faceless person he'd ever imagined telling his father that he couldn't make it, that only the rich families who'd been in the United States for generations had a right to choose their destinies and control the growth of their homes, towns, regions, states, country.

"You know, Louis, you're not really in your element here at all."

"You're right, Mark, I'm not," Louis said. "Small town. Brawn before brains. Loving the snow and ice and simple, *very* simple, repetitive pursuits."

9

RONNIE COULDN'T BELIEVE IT. She'd thought she'd dodged this bullet when, two nights ago, dessert had enforced a truce between these two.

She should have known better. Maybe she *had* known better. From the moment they'd arrived at the rink and she'd seen Mark out on the rink, skating around like some kind of elemental being with his brothers, she'd felt trouble in the air.

Both because Louis had been walking right beside her at the time and had spotted Mark at the same time—she'd felt his body stiffen—and because a part of her had responded with such a strange, atavistic longing as she'd watched Mark skating around. Something in the way he moved was just so un-city. Unselfconsciousness. Like he just *was*, with no apologies or qualifications. With Louis, despite his testosterone and determination to always get what he wanted, the route there was always carefully considered. "Whereas we want to make such and such an impression..." or "This is usually the best little bistro in the Loop, but it really depends on who's cooking tonight." Slipping and sliding towards his goal.

Mark had just as much testosterone, she was realizing, but it expressed itself differently. With him, he sometimes might not know the right thing to do, but he wouldn't make excuses if it didn't work out.

What Ronnie did not want to see right now, though, was just what Mark figured was the right way to deal with Louis's goading.

She popped to her feet and stepped awkwardly directly between Mark and Louis, her bum in Mark's face, which gave her a perverse kind of thrill. "Yeah, I don't think this is going to happen, Louis. You can't come into this town, into my family's house, come out on a family outing, then start insulting us."

Louis had shook his head at her when she'd stood up and it looked like he'd actually been about to push her to one side before he thought better of it. "I wasn't insulting you," he snapped out. "I was insulting the Neanderthal who tripped you and dragged you down onto the ice."

"A minute ago, you said you were going to thank him for saving me."

He gave her a withering look. "Out of your depth here, hon."

"Out of my *depth?*"

"Can we discuss this later? Maybe back in Chicago when you're picking out an expensive wedding dress or registering us at Pottery Barn or Tiffany's?"

"You honestly think you can order me around like this? You came out all this way to win me back and that's what you think?"

Louis gave a little sigh and reached out to hold her by her

upper arms like he was restraining a baby. Because she was wearing skates and he wasn't, it didn't have quite the effect it usually did, when he towered over her, looking down. Now she was almost eye to eye with him and it wasn't, she realized, a pretty sight.

"Ronnie, look. I did chase after you because I'd been a putz. Stupid. I was in the wrong. My bad, so my turn to grovel a little. Which I did. Which I've been doing since I got here. I've been digging out snowbanks and taking pictures of your family outing. But let's be realistic here. You love me. Or at least you want to, because marrying me just makes so much sense for you. For both of us. We match. You're talented and beautiful. I'm smart, driven, and rich. We're both big city people, either Chicago or elsewhere. Maybe New York if my firm sends me there. I can give you a life you've always aspired to. I want to give you that life. And really all I'm asking is a little respect here. I want you to be smiling at *me* when I'm around. I want you to give my proposal the consideration it deserves and not leave me hanging. I want you, when some small town gomer you went to school with comes around and tries to seduce you, to just tell him—"

He was cut off by a gloved hand grabbing his shoulder from behind and whirling him half around. Mark! Up from his chair without Ronnie feeling it!

"This gomer's had just about enough of you," Mark said. "Take off the camera."

"Really?" Louis said.

"My dad's camera!" Ronnie cried without thinking.

Louis shrugged it off his neck, handed it to her, then turned to face Mark again. Mark shoved him backwards before he got squared up.

It wasn't towards the rink, thankfully, just sideways, off the carpets and shoveled-down area of snow out across the deeper snow of the field, but Louis stumbled anyway, went down onto his bum in the snow, then rolled up, shaking off snow and spitting mad.

His gloved hands came up in front of him, but not like a boxer, more like Bruce Lee. And Ronnie tried to remember desperately if Louis had actually studied any martial arts. He went to the gym all the time and was in fantastic physical shape. She knew that. And he had killer instincts. But had she ever seen him actually punch anyone?

"Mark, don't!" she called out. "And you don't either, Louis. Stop this now!"

But Mark had apparently gone as stupid as Louis. Still wearing skates, he'd stepped out after his adversary and his blades and feet and leg up to his mid-calf disappeared into the snow. He looked taller than he should have because of the skates, at least as tall as Louis. And definitely broader. Like some kind of elevated gorilla to Louis's sleek tiger.

"Hey!" came a cry from the ice. Followed by other voices. "What!" "Mark!" "Who's that—?" "What're they—?" And the Stephanopolus kids' excited chant of, "Fight! Fight! Fight!"

Suddenly Louis had scooped up a crusty lump of snow

he'd found and flung it at Mark, who batted it aside. Louis laughed and backed away, taunting. "Come on, skater boy! School boy! Daddy's boy! Come and get me!"

Then Louis danced backwards in his boots through the snow. Not gracefully. It was too deep for that. But more gracefully than Mark could come after him in his skates.

Then Mark was running forward with a roar, with big leaping strides to clear his skates and their blades of the deep snow with each step.

Horrified, Ronnie turned from the scene to see, she was sure, Mark's brother's running out there to rein him in. But no. They'd all just skated over to the side of the skating rink, even Suzie and Emma, and were just *watching*. Like spectators at a roadside disaster. Watch the hometown boy chase down the city boy.

But Louis was *her* city boy, whether she was ever going to marry him or not. It was because of her that he was here. And she'd spent most of her free time over the last two years of her life with him, laughing with him, confiding in him, making plans with him…

Unsure what else to do, Ronnie scrambled to find her boots then sat back down on one of the lawn chairs, put her dad's camera on the other one, and tugged off her gloves with her teeth so she could attack the already-iced-up laces of her skates. She watched the bizarre and horrible game of ape-and-tiger-in-the-snow at the same time.

Mark kept almost reaching Louis, then Louis would turn

and sprint hard to one side, puffing hard, and Mark would almost fall as he lunged sideways, grunting, to try and grab him. Both men were obviously in amazing shape because the chase had now run the good seventy yards or so over to the old equipment graveyard where the Stephanopolus wives had gone, then back towards the barns, then back towards the rink again and past it towards a copse of trees that looked like a borderline between Stony's property and his neighbor's.

By the time Ronnie finally had her boots on, Louis had led Mark back towards the rink again and Ronnie could hear both men breathing the icy air in and out like they had bad asthma. But just as Louis shot her a grin to tell her he was so in control here and loving every second of humiliating Ronnie's childhood friend, Mark surged forward with a roar and caught Louis unprepared.

The two men tumbled together down into the show, fists wailing at each other as they went. Gloves still on, but it looked to Ronnie as she plunged out through the snow towards them, like their knees and elbows and everything were being used to hit and hurt. It was hard to tell with the snow and coat flaps flying, the pair of them rolling, the deadly flash of Mark's skates making Ronnie jerk sideways as she reached them and began screaming, "Stop it! Stop it! STOP IT NOW!"

Louis seemed to hear her first and pull his head back from the melee. Mark, his face an ugly mask of rage, took the opportunity to land a solid right to Louis's jaw, snapping the latter's head sideways so Louis fell back to the snow.

Then Mark, chest heaving, half fell on top of him, but went no further. He held himself there a moment, staring at the groaning Louis. Then he rolled sideways off him, pushed himself up enough to get his skates back under him, and did an awkward high-footed limp back to the lawn chairs. He didn't look at Ronnie as he went.

The two Stephanopolus young boys and Nick started cheering but were silenced by their fathers.

Without looking at anyone, Mark sat on a lawn chair that creaked under his weight, tugged off his gloves, and started undoing his laces. As he did so, Ronnie finally took a big gulp of air and ran over to where Louis still lay, groaning, in the snow. When she got there she dropped down to her knees beside him, feeling the cold of the snow slowly soak through her jeans and long underwear. What Louis had done, she almost understood. She'd seen him verbally attack enough people before. But what Mark had done really shook her. It made her question what she thought she knew about him. Or about all men?

Louis looked up at her through slitted eyes and gave a half grin.

"Brawn over brains," he croaked. "Primitive upbringing beats...unh...time in the gym."

"Sst!" Ronnie pressed a finger to his lips. "Don't make me leave you here."

A tromping sound behind her made her turn and she was shaken to see Mark standing behind her, face still sweaty, but now wearing his boots and wearing a mask of blank-faced calm.

"Beauchamps," he said to Louis, and Ronnie was shocked he even remembered Louis's last name, "you're a hell of a runner and fighter." He leaned forward and stuck down a gloved hand towards Louis.

Louis looked at it for a second, his eyes flicking with calculation. Then he said, "You too, Stephanopolus. With a mean right hook."

He took the proffered hand and Mark pulled him up to his feet, leaving Ronnie, still on her knees, reeling as she stared up at the two men and tried to figure out how aliens had somehow switched places with them.

Or maybe, to go back to that book her mom had always been trying to get her to read when she was in high school, men really were from a different planet—Mars, home of the warriors.

She was still shaking her head when Louis reached down a hand and helped her to her feet. As the three of them walked back to the lawn chairs, all of the hockey players except for Alex and Stephano returned to skating. The three Stephanopolus wives, with two young children who had to be the offspring of the youngest Stephanopolus brother, were also converging on the lawn chair area, coming down the path from the farm house. They must have been exploring or getting hot chocolate.

When Ronnie, Mark, and Louis reached the chairs area, Stephano started in with a quick apology to Ronnie for setting her up for the collision with Mark. Then the Stephanopolus wives, both breathtakingly beautiful in different ways, arrived with their charges and Mark did introductions all around. The two little ones, who actually looked only about a year or two younger than Nick, obviously liked all this about as much as high tea. Before anyone could stop them, they ran, slipping and sliding, out onto the ice.

The hockey game screeched to another halt. Stony called it a day. Everyone skated off the ice.

It made such a crowd in the little chairs area, that Alex grabbed the camera and dragged Ronnie and Nick back out onto the ice. They were followed by the eleven and twelve-year-old Stephanopolus boys who started skating backwards, dragging the two younger Stephanopolus cousins around on their boots, the younger ones screeching in glee.

"You sure do like 'em feisty," Ronnie's younger brother said to her as they watched and he snapped pictures.

"What?"

Alex laughed. "I'm talking about the two back there." He nodded to the crowd that was milling about off the side of the rink, trying to find their boots in the midst of chaos. "The big ones who were punching each other out over who gets to kiss you."

"Mark's never kissed me!" Ronnie said, then blushed, wishing she hadn't said that.

"Really? How come?"

Ronnie felt her face get even hotter. This was getting to be an annoyingly regular thing wherever Mark was concerned. "Maybe because he doesn't want to."

Alex gave a little snort.

"Or because *I* don't want to."

A bigger snort.

"Or because it just wouldn't be a very smart thing to do with someone I've barely met when I've got a guy who wants to marry me staying in the same house with me and you and Mom and Dad and the whole family!"

Alex nodded. "Closer."

Ronnie looked at him. She looked at the crowd on the side of the rink, where Mark and Louis now seemed to be getting along like the best of friends, talking and joking, describing things to each other with gestures, probably to be understood over the rest of the little crowd. Ronnie looked back at Alex and just shrugged in bewilderment.

"No opportunity?" she said.

Alex laughed and pointed at her. "Now we're getting it! Which is why I had a little discussion with Stephano earlier."

"Oh no. What is this? Youngest brothers unite?"

"Something like that. We got bossed around so much by you guys when we were little that we figure it's payback time."

"What?"

"Did I say 'bossed around'? I meant helped out, looked after, affectionately guided. That's what we're doing with you two, anyway. You and Mark."

"Uh-hunh. And we should listen to you why?"

Alex leaned his head forward and looked at her with raised eyebrows like some of the more impatient professors she remembered from university. "Look at my wife and kids, Ronnie. Look at Stephano's. We may not be the smartest or most successful of the people here, but we're smart in love, okay?"

Given what Ronnie remembered of Alex's courtship of Suzie, she had to grin at that, but decided to save her younger brother's dignity by not laughing in his face. Besides, he *had* ended up with Suzie. And it was probably the best single thing he ever could have done in his life. And Stephano's wife, Yasmine... How had a small town boy like Stephano ended up with an exotic, charming woman like that? True, these were only Ronnie's first impressions, but she'd been instantly blown away not only by Yasmine's beauty, but by her instant warmth and the way she'd taken Ronnie's hand like she understood every confusing thing that was going through Ronnie's mind about what had just happened, and that it was all okay. That it was okay to be confused, and that it would all work out.

She looked barely in her twenties and Ronnie still immediately wanted to be like her when she grew up.

"So you and Stephano were talking..." she prompted.

Alex grinned in the way he had that made him look like a faerie prince. Probably what had won him Suzie way back when. "Okay," he told Ronnie. "We worked out a very simple plan..."

~~~~

Later, when they'd said their goodbyes all around, with tentative plans for a rematch on New Year's Day, and everyone had piled back into their vehicles to head back to their respective family homes, Ronnie turned to Louis as he drove the borrowed Land Rover. Louis had the radio up on a soft pop station and Emma and Jeff were having an intense murmured conversation in the back seat. Ronnie spoke low enough that she hoped her voice didn't carry.

"So what all did you talk about in the middle of everyone changing out of their skates?"

"Hm?" Louis glanced her way and smirked. "You mean like did we bond and become best buds?"

"From your tone of voice, I'm guessing that didn't happen."

"Let's just say we reached an understanding. Instead of trying to kill each other, we'd both just lay off you for a bit, give you some space, let things cool down. Then, when you're in your right mind and make the obvious choice…"

"Meaning marrying you, of course."

He shrugged like it was a given. "We agreed we both wanted what was best for you, but it has to be your choice."

"How very magnanimous of you."

"And of Mark."

"Him too."

They drove on without speaking for a minute, then

Ronnie said, "What does that mean, exactly? That you were both going to lay off me for a bit?"

Louis glanced at her then back to the road. "I have to leave this afternoon. I need to drive back to Chicago for a few days to deal with things. Mark agreed on his small-town honor—gotta love it—that he wouldn't call you or 'arrange' to be someplace you regularly go while I'm gone."

"I see. You were making sure I stay chaste while you go back to work."

He raised his eyebrows. "Whew. If just seeing him is that risky, then yeah. I guess so. Let the Christmas buzz wear off and really think practically about what you want in life, okay? I'll be back for New Year's Eve, then we'll drive back to Chicago together New Year's Day. Start a new year, a new life together..."

"What are you going back to Chicago for?"

He looked sideways at her. "I told you. Work."

"Urgent work, if you're willing to risk losing me."

He frowned and glanced at the couple in the back who were still leaned together in their intense conversation. He subtly turned the radio up louder and leaned a bit sideways to speak quietly to Ronnie. "If you have to know, it involves Mayville. That company I'm working with that's competing for a bid in a nearby town? They have their eye on things here too. There's a big furniture company that may be moving its production facilities here and my client sees major growth happening. Something your dad and everyone else here seems pretty dead set against."

Ronnie felt herself go pale. "Woodwand International," she murmured.

Louis jerked a little and shot her a piercing look. "Where did you hear that name?"

"Uh…"

Louis glanced at the oblivious couple in the back seat then fixed his gaze on Ronnie so intently that she worried he was going to drive them off the road. "*Where?*"

"Mark," she blurted and instantly regretted it. It felt like she'd betrayed a confidence she didn't even know she was supposed to keep. "He…he knows about Woodwand. I got the impression that lots of people do. It's not that big a secret."

Louis studied her a beat longer then looked back to the road, correcting a slight drift of the Land Rover to avoid sliding into a ditch. "You're absolutely right, Ron-Ron. It's probably not that big a secret. But humor me, okay? Don't go talking about it with your father or anyone else."

"But if it's not—"

"Just don't!"

The vehemence was loud enough to actually get the attention of Emma and Jeff in the back seat. They looked up. Louis smiled back at them. "Sorry! We're almost back!"

But while Emma and Jeff seemed reassured, Ronnie felt herself sinking lower and lower in her seat, pressed down by the weight on her chest of a sudden tangle of secrets and politics that she didn't understand. Didn't *want* to understand.

Except that they involved her hometown, and her father, and Louis, and Mark, and, because Ronnie's future was getting drawn tighter and tighter to at least one of them, her.

The irony was that if Stephano and Alex came through, she might actually get a chance to ask Mark about it all.

She wasn't sure if she felt eager about that prospect, or terrified.

All she knew was that Louis couldn't leave soon enough.

10

THE DAY AFTER CHRISTMAS, even before going downstairs for the breakfast he could smell cooking, Mark gathered up the research he'd printed out on Woodwand and Stanco Bros., and his own proposal about how they could safely partner with Stanco on the Putter's Ridge project. The challenge had been to maintain the character and vision of the Gold Construction but still expand the project's scope and financial upside for everyone involved. Otherwise, he knew, Edward Stanco wouldn't even look at it. He reread the proposal and added a few more things on environmental practices and neighborhood consultation processes that bent it even more towards the GC ethic. These would be the sugar to get his father nodding, but would probably be the first things Edward Stanco would want to negotiate out, or at least weaken. The realities of business. Mark's father would understand that.

Mark went to find him.

Instead, he encountered Stephano, reading a newspaper in an armchair in the front entryway which Mark had always thought was primarily decorative in nature.

"Hey, Steph," Mark said. "Seen Dad this morning?"

Stephano looked up. "Dad? Oh yeah. Told me to tell you he wanted to meet you out at the Putter's Ridge work site whenever you got up and got breakfast. I told him to text you, but you know Pop and technology."

"Not his first instinct." Mark frowned, thinking of the website that he'd checked over after Ronnie's comment only to find she was right about all its shortcomings. Something else he'd have to fix when he came back to work here again.

But the time... He looked at his watch. Still barely nine a.m. His father had intentionally shut down the site until after New Year's. One of those wonderfully generous Gold Construction traditions—to give all their employees and work crews an extended paid break over the Christmas holiday. Why would he be up at Putter's Ridge at all during this period?

He looked back at his younger brother. "Did he say what he wanted to talk about?"

Stephano had gone back to reading the paper almost like he didn't want to catch Mark's eye. He shook his head. "No idea. But it sounded important. He got Aaron to drive him up. Left you the truck."

Which, given Stephano's behavior, meant that Mark's father had been agitated. Some financial crisis he'd been holding back on? Or had one of the Clearys passed on Mark's little revelation about Woodwand? Worst case scenario, had

Edward Stanco become so uneasy about relying on Mark that he'd gone behind Mark's back and approached Mark's father directly? *That* would not have gone well.

"Okay. What's everyone else doing? Aaron's obviously come and gone. What about Chris?" Because if there was one thing Mark had learned about all his brothers' kids was that they were up at the crack of dawn almost without exception. And while Stephano and Yasmine lived a couple towns over, so were staying in the Stephano family home like Mark for the holidays, Chris and Aaron both had their own houses in town. They'd been coming by for big family breakfasts, but their sons were rarely content to play quietly afterwards. They had to get outside somewhere. They were do-ers.

"More hockey," Stephano said. "Aaron was meeting them there. Yasmine's got our two in lock down. Twins caught a bit of a cold."

"Right." So Mark did an about-face with his collection of binders and drawings and headed to the kitchen for some quick fuel before heading out.

There he borrowed two large canvas shopping bags from his mother and loaded all the partnering materials into them, then acceded to his mother's insistence he sit down while she served him eggs and fried turkey hash. She was about to add on four huge buttermilk pancakes with homemade raspberry compote and maple syrup when he stopped her. His stomach was in knots. He was obviously more worked up about this meeting with his father than he'd thought.

She came over and pulled out a chair to sit beside him, all dusky round cheekbones, chin, and bust on a wispy body.

"Did Stephano tell you that your father wanted to meet you out at the site?"

However soft her voice might have been, Mark caught a twinkle in her eyes as she said it. Put together with something that had been in Stephano's manner...

"Mom?" he said slowly. "What's going on?"

She turned her face away and stood up, hurrying to the sink, where she'd been cleaning up when he came in. "Oh, it's nothing. Your poppy, you know..."

He opened his mouth to press, but changed his mind. The way she was acting, it didn't sound like a *bad* surprise, whatever it was. Probably a whole lot more fun that what Mark was going to deliver.

He stood and walked over behind her, kissed the top of her head, then said, "Gotta run." He grabbed his bags of binders and went for the truck.

~~~~

Craziness. That's what this was.

She'd said it before. She'd said it that very first evening when she'd found herself attracted to Mark. She'd become absolutely sure of it the next day when she'd seen him downtown and then out at this same work site she was driving up to now.

The man did things to her. Sent shivers through her. Made

her imagine she felt electric tingles from his touch. Made her question everything about her choices to leave Mayville, to work in Chicago, and, most of all, to tie herself to Louis.

But now, on top of all that, there was this Woodwand thing that Mark and Louis knew about and maybe no one else was supposed to.

Hunh. She huffed a breath of steam into the still cold air of the car as she turned out onto Port Line Highway that circled around the north end of town. As she passed the Phelps farm where they'd all played hockey yesterday, and where Mark and Louis had fought like a bunch of school kids, she shivered again. The heater in her dad's truck didn't seem to be pumping out much heat. Or at least not enough to overcome the frosty chill from outside and the sheer nerves she'd carried with her into the car after Stephano's phone call.

The clear weather that had been with them since that pre-Christmas snowstorm had welcomed in a crisp wind this morning that blew the hard edges off the sun-sparkled landscape like there was a light mist of white rising off everything.

She could feel it trying to push her dad's small pickup around as she drove.

Passing the eastern edge of town, she turned left onto Ridge Road to climb into the hills, and stomped on the gas. It was a way of avoiding her own cross-examination of herself. 55 mph on a curving, snowy road. Why, exactly had she agreed to Alex and Stephano's silly plan to get her and Mark alone together? 60 and tires slipping a bit. She could tell herself she had to clear up this Woodwand mystery, but was that really it? 65. And if it wasn't, and this attraction she felt toward Mark was mutual—70—was the passion to come really going to be worth the emotional pain when they faced the reality of their different worlds and called it off?

An almost-hairpin turn ahead woke her up with a surge of adrenaline as she braked, felt the truck start to slide, and her heart jumped into her throat. She prayed her dad kept his truck well-tuned as she stomped hard on the brake pedal and held it down. The ABS kicked in with a teeth-rumbling shudder, pulsing the brakes on and off faster than she ever could have. She turned into the skid, felt a surge of exhilaration as she regained control, and steered through the turn.

"Okay, *now* I'm warm," she muttered to herself as she slowed the car to something more befitting the driving conditions. She was actually sweating and trembling. And felt even stupider about this adventure her little brother had set her up for.

But she kept driving.

Two minutes later she pulled into the small, plowed-out lot she and the rest of her family had parked in two days ago. Seemed a lifetime.

There was only one other vehicle in the lot, a Ford Super Duty pickup truck. Oversized, powerful, spotlessly clean, owned by Mark's dad, but probably not driven by the father today. There was no one in the truck, but even as blown snow whipped and eddied around the tires, Ronnie imagined she could see steam still rising off the front engine hood. Because Stephano had told her Mark had just left when he'd called. So he'd have arrived only a few minutes before Ronnie, assumed his father was waiting for him at the site itself, and hiked down the same little trail he'd taken all the Clearys on just before Christmas.

Ronnie climbed out of her own father's smaller pickup, shut the door, gasped a bit at the icy wind, and began walking that trail.

~~~~

Mark was puzzled and not a little concerned that his father wasn't anywhere on the site that he could see. There hadn't been any snow since before Christmas when he'd done his little tour up here for Ronnie and her family, and the wind today had blown mini-drifts over all the tracks out in the parking lot, so he couldn't be sure whether another vehicle had even come up here before him. Nor were there signs that anyone had cut any new trails through the deeper snow down the foot path. Not that they'd necessarily *want* to when they could just follow the existing ones.

Standing at the door of the little controller's hut, he cupped his hands around his mouth and yelled, "Pop!" as loud as he could. But his words got sucked away the minute they left his mouth. Damn wind.

It was cold, too, which concerned him. If his father *had* come up here like Stephano said, and gone wandering to check on something… If he'd fallen… If he'd had another stroke or heart attack?

Damn it.

He bustled back inside the controller's hut, closing the door behind him. The hut was actually a good ten feet by ten feet and insulated against the cold, with only two 3x4 high-R windows to look out over the worksite and town of Mayville far down the hillside. That was important since they'd planned to work through the winter and needed a place to handle all the paperwork and comm duties that wasn't going to freeze their rear ends off. Not to mention having a place to bring in any of the on-site workers who had a bad reaction to the cold.

The hut had a long desk against the wall opposite the door where he'd spread his binders out. But more important, it had electricity. That powered lights; a fridge that held water, soft drinks, and fruit juice; a radio; and baseboard heaters. It had been ice cold when he'd arrived ten or twelve minutes ago and he'd automatically cranked up the heat. But then he'd gone outside, looking for his father, and only now questioned why his father would have come up here for a meeting without at least turning on the heat in the controller's hut.

He pulled out his cell phone again to try to call home but got barely one bar that flickered on and off. The blowing snow, he assumed. The fact that GC hadn't yet run in telephone cables drove him crazy. Everyone just assumed you'd have cell service, but of course just when you really needed it…

Okay. Think. There'd most likely been a miscommunication here. Stephano had gotten their father's message garbled about either where to meet or when. And it wasn't a huge deal. Only a short hike back to the parking area, then a ten or fifteen minute drive back to town.

It killed him that he'd gotten all worked up the whole way here about presenting his Stanco plan to his father, and now it had to wait. But it was what it was. You just accepted reality. Adjusted. Moved on.

"Except with women," he said to the empty hut as he grabbed first one binder, then another, stuffing them back into the bags he'd borrowed from his mother.

To be more precise: Except with Ronnie Cleary.

Maybe that was what was really bothering him. He wanted to clear this thing up with his dad so he could put it behind him, or at least in its proper place, and focus on what he was going to do to win the girl. Sure, she was practically engaged to a rich lawyer and wanted to live in Chicago. And sure, he'd promised that lawyer that he wouldn't go near Ronnie while the lawyer was away. (And just how had he made that promise anyway? What had he been *thinking*?) But every time he saw her, however briefly and however stupidly he behaved, he kept getting this intense feeling that he just hadn't had with any other girls or women ever. Like she was the one. He might win her or not, but *she was the one.*

He'd seen that same conviction take over all three of his

brothers and remembered the cynical way he'd discounted theirs as a simple lust reaction coupled to some romantic dreams of the kind of woman they'd always wanted.

But...Mark liked to think it wasn't that way with Ronnie at all. First, because he'd never really had any vision of the kind of woman he wanted. He'd been too busy, frankly, to make it a serious part of his plans.

Second, because—and he'd just figured this out yesterday at the skating rink—that first reason was a lie. He'd never had a vision of the *kind* of woman he wanted because a part of him had settled on the *exact* woman long ago, when they were both just kids. She'd unsettled him then. She unsettled him now. He just never realized, as a kid, what that all meant, how the changeable, sharp and funny girl she was seemed to connect directly to the solid, directed part of him. Completing the circuit. Not completing *him*; completing *them*.

And of course he had to see her again and figure this out right when his entire career plan was in crisis. What was up with that?

Stupidity. That's what.

She fit none of his career plans, was way too prickly, and was going out with someone else. And they weren't kids anymore! To really know if they fit together as adults, they had to at least touch each other! More than a handshake, more than leading her on the path from the parking lot or catching her when she crashed into him at Stony's hockey rink.

What would it be like to actually hold her when she wasn't

bundled up in serious winter gear? To feel the shape of her body? To breathe in her breath and warmth? To touch her lips with his? And to actually *talk* with her truly and deeply about her life, about his? If he just had that opportunity, he'd know for sure. And she'd know for sure.

If they just had that chance.

He was chagrined to remember Stephano confessing thoughts like that to Mark, and he remembered smiling at him and thinking, *He's such a kid.* Was it any wonder Mark was too embarrassed to share his feelings about Ronnie with his brothers?

Shaking his head ruefully, he hoisted up the bags of binders and turned to the door...

...just as the knob turned and it swung inward to reveal a shivering-but-hopeful-faced Ronnie Cleary.

"Stephano lied to you about your dad being here to meet with you!" she blurted over the howl of the wind. "It's all a setup to get the two of us alone together."

11

RONNIE FELT THE WIND WHIP AROUND HER BACK, buffeting her back and forth as she stared into the little hut with her face going red.

Good grief, what had she just done?

Just putting it out there, she argued back. *I am* not *going lie about why I'm here. I mean, what else could I say anyway? I have some business questions I want to ask you about Woodwand?*

Then Mark's look of shock dissolved into an amused smile and she wished she *had* gone with the business quiz thing.

"Close the door," he said.

"What?"

"Come in and close the door," he said, louder.

She swallowed and did. The click of the door and the resulting hush was replaced by a loud beating sound inside her own head. Her heart, she realized. Did it show? Of course it showed. Everything always showed on her face. She was the worst poker player in the world, Alex had told her, more than once. As a child, Emma would always learn her secrets by just peppering her with questions and watching her reactions, whether she answered or not.

"I didn't come out here to make out with you," she said.

"No? Then why did you come?"

"To talk. To have a chance to just talk with you. You wanted to talk the other day we were up here, I could tell. We never really had the chance. Not at that hockey party either."

He snorted. "No, I was too busy there being a jackass with your boyfriend."

"Don't call him that."

"He's not your boyfriend?"

"No, it's just... He has been. We're trying to work out exactly what we are right now."

She hadn't moved from the door since she'd closed it and he hadn't approached her, she noted. Giving her space. Good. He was good. Sensitive. Louis never would have done that. Never had. He'd always just barged into her space and claimed it. From the very first day she'd seen him at that gala charity dinner she'd been helping to cater with Rolf and Chester. And Ronnie had *let* Louis just barge in because she'd figured it showed how manly and powerful he was...

Now, considering her seriously, Mark slowly set down on the floor the two heavy-looking shopping bags he'd been holding by their handles, and he stepped back to sit on the edge of the desk.

"What are the issues?" he asked.

"About what?"

"You and Louis. Did he pull back or did you?"

Ronnie jammed her hands into her jacket pockets. "He cheated on me. I called him on it. He said let's break up. Then he followed me out here, apologized, and proposed marriage."

She looked down. Wow, had she just really blabbed all that? Mark asks her a question and she just answers? Honestly? What was that all about?

"That…has to be a bit difficult," Mark said evenly.

Her turn to snort. "You think?"

"Explains a lot, though."

"Like?"

"Like how you could seem so approachable. How you seemed to be drawn to me almost as much as I was drawn to you."

Oh, jeez. There went her face coloring again. "What? You don't think it was just your irresistible charm?"

He shook his head. "I'm not that charming."

"Don't sell yourself short."

"Okay." He gave a little self-deprecating nod. "I'll allow that you find me charming. At least a little. Which makes me wonder a bit about your judgment, but I like it."

"Wow. Are you sure you're not a lawyer in disguise? I don't know how I'd even begin to attack that one."

"It wasn't meant as some kind of trick," he said and pushed off from the desk to move on a line almost sideways to her, getting closer without approaching directly. Ronnie felt her heart rate increase almost a beat faster for every foot closer. And this even though he was dressed in a drab olive workman's parka today. None of his splendid body shape was visible, but his face, his liquid brown eyes and dark curly hair, his *presence* when he moved, were enough to get all sort of unfamiliar feelings zinging through her.

"Just stop there," she said and held up a hand. Licked her lips.

"Okay." He did. "Look, Ronnie. You obviously know I find you attractive. Of course I find you attractive. Any male with a pulse would find you attractive. But there's something more, as well. That I liked even as a kid. Maybe the fact you don't hide who you are."

"There's not a lot to hide. I'm just…me."

He looked down at the floor like he didn't know what to say, how to keep this conversation going. So Ronnie volunteered. And not just to keep the conversation going, she realized. She wanted Mark to really know who she was so that he could judge her just like Louis had judged her. No false fronts. No going in with one idea then getting disappointed.

"I started going to university in computer science and web design," she said, "because I could. I liked the artistic part of it. And it was supposed to be a real career. Safe. But it turned out to be just…okay. So I dropped out to work in a candy shop."

"Not just any candy shop. The best candy shop in—"

"No! I'm not talking about Chester's Sweets. I dropped out to work in a little place called Londoner Chocolates. And it wasn't even because I loved chocolate or any kind of candy.

It was because I needed a job. I'd…lost my way. I didn't want to be a computer geek. I knew I wasn't going to be a lawyer or an English professor or whatever. So I quit. I dropped out two credits shy of graduating. My folks just about had aneurysms." She clapped her hand over her mouth, mortified. "Sorry. That's stupid of me. My mouth is running off with me."

Mark shook his head. "It's okay. Really. Your dropping out of school didn't cause my dad's stress. But how did you end up at Chester's then?"

Ronnie wrapped her arms around herself. She'd borrowed Emma's puffy white ski jacket to come out here. It wasn't a perfect fit, but it was slimmer, more body flattering, than Ronnie's own. Underneath it, she had on a simple, forest green top that was even slinkier. She normally wore it as a base under a sweater or blouse, but not this time. Because if this was going to be her one chance to get physical with Mark Stephanopolus, she wanted to make sure she sealed the deal. From her end, at least.

Or that, despite this Woodwand thing, *had* been her plan.

Now, here she was, choosing to give him all the dirt about her career stumbles and what Louis described as her chronic lack of direction in life. Her earlier plan of being all cool and sexy and in control was pretty much toast.

"Chester's?" She quirked up the corner of her mouth. "Well, about three months into my time at Londoner Chocolates, I had this epiphany. I realized, as I stood there stirring up a big vat of special ganache that we were going to shape into a group of cute critters I had come up with, I was enjoying the hell out of my job. It had meaning. It gave joy to others. And I was good at it."

Just the memory of that revelation brought a remembered flood of joy and she sprung her arms open wide for a second before remembering where she was and wrapping them defensively around herself again.

"Go on," Mark said. He leaned forward towards her, apparently really wanting to get this story.

Ronnie shrugged. "One day I'm working away in the back, doing the hand-decoration on that same set of little animal truffles I had come up with earlier, doing their little faces and ears or claws, Mr. Southy, who runs Londoners, comes barging into the back, his face all red, and he's followed by this big, roly-poly guy who's smiling and looking around and drawing in these deep breaths like he wants to inhale our entire kitchen."

"Chester?"

She shook her head. "Chester's the businessman. This is Rolf, the chocolatier. Maybe the single best chocolatier in America." She felt her surge of pride as she said it, like Rolf was family—the big gay brother she'd never had. "Of course, I didn't know it then. He just looked like a big happy, chocolate-hungry guy."

"Hungry for your chocolates."

"Exactly! Because the chocolatier in charge when I was hired had accepted an offer to go to Paris, so I'd pretty much taken over all the chocolate recipes by then. I had two assistants, but I was doing the actual recipes. Experimenting. Writing down the ones that worked. Building a kind of personal cookbook. And business was up. Mr. Southy was happy."

"Hence the visit from the competition."

"I guess." Ronnie stopped and thought about that. She'd actually never processed Rolf's visit in that light. She'd always just assumed he'd heard about her work and wanted to meet a fellow chocolatier. The competitive economics hadn't occurred to her.

"Which is why your boss was so angry."

"Mr. Southy," Ronnie blinked as she remembered. "My gosh. I thought I'd ticked him off. Something I'd done…"

"It was something you'd done, all right. You'd become a valuable asset that the competition wanted to steal."

"And I let them steal me," Ronnie said slowly.

"Did Mr. Southy offer you a raise?"

Ronnie looked at Mark, seeing just how beautiful he was, his jaw all square, his eyes eating her up. He seemed closer than before. "He did. The very next day. Before Rolf brought Chester back to visit me and take me to tour their little shop. Mr. Southy wanted me to commit to a five-year deal and Londoner owning all my recipes."

Mark shook his head, smiling. "Must have offered you a lot of money for that."

"Hm? Oh. Yeah. It was a pretty nice figure, I guess."

"And what did Rolf and Chester offer you that topped it?"

Ronnie met Mark's smile and felt it light one of her own. "Freedom," she said. "Profit sharing. Working with Rolf. And by the time they did their whole song and dance for me, I'd done a little research. I knew who I'd get to be working alongside, who I'd be learning from. Did you know Rolf won the World Chocolate Masters? Twice. Only chocolatier who's ever done that."

"So far."

"Of course. Oh!" She caught his implication and blushed. "Except that I'm not specializing in chocolates anymore."

"Rolf didn't want the competition? Worried you might open up your own shop?"

"No! I mean, that's not it. When I joined Chester's, they gave me the choice of what I wanted to work on. I took over their brittle making, marzipan, and soft candies."

"Which I bet has been booming."

She grinned. "It's been doing okay. They also let me redesign their website and rejig their charitable donations plan. A little candy making, a little of the other stuff…"

"So you're well rounded."

Her grin turned into a dry-mouthed swallow. Mark, she realized, had somehow managed to move closer and closer to her while she'd been caught up in her story. Now he was barely a foot away. And, maybe it was because she'd been inside this heated hut for a good ten minutes or so now, but Ronnie suddenly felt like she was burning up.

Mark reached out a hand and touched her cheek lightly with the fingers. Oh, goodness, the electricity there. Her legs felt a little unsteady and she leaned back against the inside wall, dropping her hands to press back against it for support.

"I believe," Mark said, following her, "that when a person is very talented in something *and* enjoys it, they should go after it with all their heart and soul."

"Even if," Ronnie said, licking her lips, "no one else takes it seriously?"

His fingers traced down her cheek to her chin as he moved in closer. The heat she felt wasn't all the room. His nose was brushing hers. His body seemed to hover just an inch from hers at all points and she could smell his skin now, a scrubbed-clean woodsy scent. It started a thrumming inside her.

"Is it important that your life be serious?" he murmured.

"Yes," she gasped. "It is. I need to believe—"

His lips cut her off, softly but intensely as her own lips responded. It was heat to heat, mouths opening, tongues exploring, and her hands left the wall behind her almost of their own accord to wrap around Mark's body, only to be frustrated by the thick stiffness of his winter workman's coat.

She grunted in annoyance, bringing her hands around to his front, in between them, searching for his coat zipper. And he finally got it, drawing back and unzipping his coat. Tossing it away from him to reveal his jeans and a tight fawn sweater with apparently nothing under it. Even as Ronnie unzipped her own borrowed jacket and shrugged out of it.

Mark's look, his hungry up and down with expanding pupils, told her all she needed to know about her choice of tops.

"Come back here," she ordered.

And when he did, she wrapped herself around him with abandon, the fingers of one hand in his hair as she kissed him, the fingers of the other clutching tightly to a shoulder that felt as solid as the earth itself. She gave a little yelp as his hands clasped her tightly around her buttocks and pulled her tightly to him.

Then she let herself flow into it.

So different from her physicality with Louis where it was always her accommodating him, trying hard to believe she loved every second because Louis had so much masculine drive and success, was so much of everything she'd always wanted, that her body *should* respond.

Oh! Mark's hand over her breast. It was like she could feel the need of him through her brassiere, through her top, and her entire body responded to that basic need with an equally intense need of its own. He sucked something up from the very core of her that shot through her spine, her legs, her arms, her fingers, her lips, even the tips of her eyelids brushing against him as they kissed.

It thrummed. It sang within her. It pulsed and rippled and zinged through her. And even though a part of her kept asking *Why this fast? Why this man?* All the rest of her said

Shut up! That he was the best of Louis, but with a small town heart, and ethics, and…

Mark pulled back for a second, breathing hard, to look at her. "This is…sudden," he breathed.

"Yes!" *Don't stop!*

"But do you want to…?"

She reached down both hands, grabbed the bottom of her top and dragged it up and off her.

12

FORTY MINUTES LATER, as the two of them lay tangled together on top of his coat and clothing, Mark felt something bubbling up inside him that he hadn't felt in so long he almost didn't recognize it. When he did, he began to laugh.

"What is it?" Ronnie said, rolling off him just enough to prop herself up and look him dead in the eyes. She didn't look worried or defensive, though. Just beautiful. Glowing. Her tangle of red curls around her head seemed to shine in the white winter light that still blared in through the steamed-up windows. Her skin, all flushed and sweaty in places, was a complement to the hair. And the lips. And the eyes. Her hair smelled like apples; the rest, like roses and musk.

But oh the *feel* of that skin of hers, its private places revealed to him, its smooth warmth shared…

He chuckled again.

"You know you want to tell me," Ronnie said, lowering her brows at him with mock severity. "Because I truly cannot bear being laughed at."

"Because your life is so serious," he said.

"It *is!*" she said. "You don't know."

"Tell me," he said and rolled up onto an elbow to study her more completely.

She saw his gaze wandering over her and blushed, but didn't cover up. For which he sent out another quick prayer of thanks. Such beauty should never be covered. In front of him, at least. When they were alone.

"It doesn't much look like you're interested in my words right now," Ronnie said, looking pointedly at the part of his body that was responding with surprising resilience to her nakedness.

"Hm. This is actually a struggle. Because honestly my mind and heart really want to know everything they can discover about you right this moment. My body has other ideas. I think I'm going to have to let you make the call on this one."

So twenty minutes later…

Now they were even sweatier, the windows steamier, but at least some of what Mark realized had been a growing, ever-present tension in his body since he'd first met Ronnie at the Cleary pre-Christmas dinner had eased. As he lay now with her lying half on top of him, her head on his chest, her fingers playing with his hair, the feeling that had made him laugh earlier was incredibly still there. He wondered whether he should share it with her.

"You want to know what I have to be serious about?" Ronnie said suddenly, her jaw moving against his breastbone, her words making his chest hair hum.

"Tell me." His free hand went to her hair now, smooth it away from her face. Such a beautiful face.

"My boyfriend."

"Your boyfriend? Are you talking about Louis?"

She nodded against his chest, saying nothing.

"Isn't that a little…over now? I mean, with all of this?"

There was a long pause, then Ronnie sighed under his hand. He could feel it all the way down her body. "It should be, shouldn't it. For more reasons than you know. But, the thing is, it's exactly for those reasons that it can't be done yet, you know?"

Mark felt a blackness building up inside him and tried to force it down. "What reasons?"

She craned her neck to look up at him. "It's complicated."

"So?"

"So I'd like to get dressed first. I think that would be easier."

The blackness ballooned inside Mark all at once and he nodded. "Sure."

As soon as she rolled off him to grab her clothes, he rolled away too, not looking at her. He felt, as he tugged on his underwear, his jeans, his socks and sweater and boots, like he'd just been kicked in the testicles. Which was, in the circumstances, kind of like having someone kick an already squeezed-dry sack.

Very pleasant image, Mark. Thank you for that.

"Okay," Ronnie said, much too quickly.

He looked and she was completely dressed again. Everything but the white puffy jacket she'd worn. Which meant he could still see far too much of the shape of her. And it was almost like he had synesthesia. He looked at her body and could simultaneously feel it, taste it, hear the sounds from her mouth, from the whisper of them being together.

It was a feeling that he'd foolishly thought he could somehow keep going forever.

"Okay," he said as he walked to the desk and sat against the edge of it again. "Explain."

~~~~

The coldness of his voice almost blocked up Ronnie's throat. Not that she had the right to expect anything else. The way she'd responded to him... Forget that. The way she'd basically thrown herself at him from the moment he'd kissed her—it was only right that he expected it meant something. She would have been very disturbed, in fact, if he *hadn't* thought that. Probably as disturbed as Mark was sounding right now.

"What you have to understand," Ronnie said, thinking hard about how best to get into this, "is that I love my family to bits."

Mark said nothing. Just watched her, hands wrapped around the edge of the desk where he sat. Waiting.

"I love them to bits. Absolutely can't live with them anymore, but I also could never let anything bad happen to them if it was in my power to stop it. And this town is their lives. My mom and dad met here in their teens, though my mom was actually born a couple towns over. They married here. They raised a family here, me and my sibs. And, like you heard, now that my dad's semi-retired, he's planning to run for City Council, to give back to the town that's given so much to him."

She thought she saw a little flicker in Mark's eyes as she talked, but nothing changed on his face. That was how he was going to play this? Like he had no emotional investment in what she was saying? Like he was just an impassive listener? Couldn't he see how this was killing her? That all she really wanted to do was tear off all her clothes again and pull him back down to the floor with her?

But she had to know. *Had* to.

"Tell me about Woodwand," she said.

This time there was a visible flinch and a narrowing of his brows. Not guilt, exactly. But something. He knew something he wasn't saying.

So she pushed harder. "Well?"

"What about it?" he said slowly. "I told you just about everything I know about them. They're probably planning to move their manufacturing base to Mayville, just outside of town. I'd guess the south end of town, taking over that small industrial park that's already there."

"And?"

"And I know your dad's not keen on any kind of big development in the town, but towns need some kind of sustainable industry to stay healthy. Has your dad talked to you about how Mayville's been doing? Its finances?"

She shook her head.

"Well I can tell you that overall it's been contracting. The only reason my dad's construction company has survived is because he's made it much more regional. If he had to rely on just Mayville for projects…" Mark squinted at the sunny, east-facing window. "You know that a lot of Midwestern towns shrank during this last recession. A couple out and out died. Businesses closed. Head offices shut down."

Ronnie was surprised by the way that made her breathing high and light in her chest. "You're saying that could happen to Mayville?"

"I'm saying that industry and development, properly managed, is a good thing for towns. And you heard my spiel on Woodwand. They're about as small-town friendly as you can get."

He hadn't moved during this whole speech, which was so out of character with his general physicality, his masculine presence, that Ronnie was sure there was more he wasn't saying. But she couldn't figure out what it would be. This was so not her area. Unless…

She raised her chin. "Have *you* made some sort of side deal with Woodwand?"

Again that barely noticeable flinch. "No," he said.

"But what? You wanted to?"

"What? No? Why are you even asking me about this?"

He might have been hiding it back before but Mark's anger was visible on his face now. And Ronnie suddenly had a flash of him tearing after Louis out on the snowfields around Stony Phelp's hockey rink. There, at least, there were witnesses to stop him from seriously beating up Louis if he lost control. No one here in this hut with them now. Just crazy little Ronnie Cleary, goading and poking at a man she knew was hiding something. Not that she could believe he'd ever lose control with her. Not in anger, at least. And that was the crazy thing. They were *connected*. He had to feel that. He'd said that. So why was he brooding and raging over there with some kind of secret keeping them apart? Why couldn't he just *tell* her?

Or was the fact that he couldn't because the secret was so bad, even worse than she was imagining, that he knew it would end everything between them? Would have to end it.

All the more reason to force it out of him here and now so they could deal with it.

She looked pointedly at the two bags of what looked like books and loose-leaf papers just a foot away from his feet, where he'd dropped them before moving in on her, kissing her, making love to her.

"Those bags," she said. "Do they have stuff you were going to discuss with your dad about your plans?"

He frowned hard and looked down at the bags, back to her. "They're…plans for Gold Construction. Yes."

"Plans for what?"

"This project. Putter's Ridge."

"Can I see them?"

"No, you may not. They're confidential. And speculative."

Ronnie folded her arms across her chest. "Just who do you think I'm going to reveal your secrets too?"

His eyes narrowed. "Let me see, a father running for town council, a boyfriend who's a corporate lawyer and would like nothing more than to see both me and my father's business fail…"

"Okay, don't call him that. My 'boyfriend.'"

"No?" Mark pushed himself up off the desk and took two steps towards her, his face flushed. "That's what you called him five minutes ago. And if he's not that, then what is he to you? How can you make love to me one minute and then grill me about business practices the next? What is going on here, Ronnie?"

She took a step back. "I am trying to sort things out, okay?" *Just talk to me!*

"How? By quizzing me to see if I'm marriage material? Was that what our little fling on the floor was too? Some kind of entrance exam? Did I pass that, at least?"

"How dare you!" *You didn't just pass. You blew the test to pieces! Weren't you paying attention?*

"How dare I? You're the one who got my brother—and

mother?—to set up this little meeting here between us. And then you start grilling me after? At least I'm being honest about how I feel about you!"

"Oh yeah? And how is that?" *Tell me! Tell me that much at least! Say it!*

"I'm… I'm… Dammit! You know what? You were right all along. This obviously could never work. Because I'm just your small town boy who's sticking around this town to look after his father. While you, for all your words of loving your family, can't wait to get away from them to Chicago!"

"Because my *job* is there!" *Ask me to stay!*

"It could be here!"

"What?"

"Just set up a shop. Call it Ronnie's! Use your social media skills to get people coming to it from all over!"

"So easy!" *No no no no…*

"Nothing's easy, Ronnie! Nothing! There's only good choices and bad ones. And maybe you need to put a little more time in figuring out just what your choices really are!"

Oh, she wanted to slam him. She wanted to punch him right in that angry face of his and shout that she couldn't make choices when she didn't even know what she was choosing! When he wouldn't tell her this big, horrible secret that he was holding between them. And then she wanted to say *Yes! Yes, of course I could make that work!* Whatever his secret was, she'd forgive him ahead of time if he could just tell her what he'd almost told her about how he felt. What he *had* told her with his body. And she wanted to jump his bones again. Answer her pounding blood. His tense, throbbing body. She wanted to jump on him and ravish him and pretend that nothing else mattered. And she'd tell him with her body what she was having trouble committing to with her words. She'd be in charge, proving to him that she did too know what she wanted. She knew exactly what.

But…

Damn it. But…

She felt herself deflate inside no matter how much she tried to pump herself into at least making this one small choice to leap at him and kiss him and…

The cold, hard realities would still be there. She might be cinnamon hot for him, but there was still her family, still her career, still the realities of the world and right and wrong. And just like she'd finally come to her senses about Louis's lack of compassion for others, she knew she couldn't blindly follow Mark if he was doing something unethical that would hurt everything she believed in.

The way she'd then cut Mark off emotionally and grilled him about his business ethics? That had been a choice. Not an impulse. Not a mistake.

"You know," she said, "after all my time with Louis, I think I can finally tell when someone's dodging a question. Or hiding things from me. Which is pretty much the same thing as lying to me. So are you going to lie to me, or come clean, Mark?"

He stared at her long and hard and she thought she saw indecision tearing back and forth across his face. Until the features hardened.

"I guess you're right not to trust me," he said. "Though why you'd trust someone like Louis ahead of me is profoundly disturbing."

"At least he's not asking me to leave Chicago."

"There is that."

Mark held her eyes a moment longer, then shook his head dismissively and reached down to the floor where he'd thrown his coat earlier. He shrugged it on and bent to pick up his two bags of what Ronnie could now see were binders, four of them, filled with papers. Nothing lightweight about whatever Mark had been planning to discuss with his dad.

"I think we're done here," he said.

He looked at her pointedly and she finally got the hint. She grabbed her own coat, Emma's coat, and tugged it on. Zipped it up.

"Quite an afternoon," she quipped at him. Getting no reaction but a sullen stare, she finally grimaced, turned, grabbed the doorknob, and let herself out. She didn't wait for him but trudged straight back the path to her dad's truck, fumbled the keys out of her jacket pocket, and climbed in.

Her eyes were streaming as she drove out of the lot.

13

FOR HIS PART, Mark was cursing and stomping at the snow when he finally followed Ronnie back along the path to the parking area.

At least part of his anger, he knew, was against himself. Because he'd let himself get ethically compromised, at least potentially, and taken far too long to face up to it and work through the issue. And while he thought he'd pretty much figured things out now, he still had to reach some kind of understanding with his father—he owed him that—before he disclosed his position to anyone else, even Ronnie.

Which meant he'd stuck himself in a bad place with her. With some women, playing his cards close to his chest might not matter, might almost be expected. With Ronnie, emotionally volatile but painfully honest in her dealings with others, playing your cards close meant you couldn't be trusted.

Dammit!

He almost considered running after her to grab her and explain a little bit of that. To tell her to be patient with him; he'd reveal everything as soon as he was able.

But part of him that was still smarting over having her make love to him then turn around and talk about Louis Beauchamps. How she could ever have chosen to go out with a guy like that... It dragged his feet back. And before he could put that aside, he heard the engine of whatever vehicle she'd driven here in roar to life and drive away.

Great. Well done, Egghead.

It was probably for the best, though. He really did need to sort things out with his father, see whether he could broker an acceptable deal between him and Edward Stanco, take care of that mess one way or another. Then he'd be in a proper place to approach Ronnie again. From a place of total honesty and full disclosure.

He smiled grimly. He also had to have a little talk with his younger brother. Let him know he appreciated the thought, but could really use a little more of a heads up the next time he tried to meddle in Mark's love life.

First though, Mark's father. He reached the Super Duty and climbed in, pretty sure where he'd find him.

~~~~

A couple blocks before she'd reached her folks' house, Ronnie pulled the pickup over to the side of the road and sat for a moment, trembling.

What had she done? Why was she so impulsive? Why was she so difficult?

Impulsive in following her desire, no, her *need*, to have some private time with Mark. Had that been simple lust? Heaven knew he had all the qualities to inspire it, both physically and character wise. He was exactly the sort of man's man she'd grown up in small-town Mayville fantasizing about. Strong, masculine, self-controlled, ultra-competent, good with his hands (oh, my, was he ever).

But then she'd gone to university and a job in the big city and found a whole new type of man to ogle—the super-smart, business savvy, sophisticate. Louis.

What scared her was how thoroughly she'd thought she belonged with Louis right up until the time she'd found out he was cheating on her. Then she'd run back here for Christmas and found Mark, the antithesis of Louis at least on the moral, straightforward, always honest and up-front scale. Or so she'd thought.

Was she just rebounding with Mark? Was that all her sudden passion for him was? It felt like more. He seemed to touch something in her that was immediate and pure. But how could she be sure? She'd just shown herself to be a wildly emotional flake. She'd had sex with him, twice in the space of a couple hours, then promptly declared her mistrust of Mark and attachment to Louis.

What was that? What? Why should Mark ever even look at her again? If he was smart, he'd run the other way screaming. (Except that Mark would never scream. He'd just stomp off, jaw set.)

Almost without realizing it, she had her cell phone in her hand, dialing one of a very small set of numbers she knew by heart. After a beat, the phone rang on the other end. And rang. And rang. Finally there was the sound of the call being transferred, and the very familiar voice of Louis's secretary answered.

"Hi, Ronnie. What can I do for you? Louis is in out-of-office meetings all day today."

Sitting hunched over in her dad's truck, wearing her sister's ski jacket, parked on a tiny road that seemed taken from another life even though she'd walked, run, and driven over it hundreds or thousands of times growing up, Ronnie didn't know what to say. She looked out over the snowy landscape of the road and realized she could even identify who lived in each of the houses on this block. Assuming no one had moved in the last few years. But in Mayville, people rarely did. Kids left home. People died. But family homes remained remarkably static. Which she guessed said something about people liking where they were.

Or just becoming too ossified to try to try something new?

"Merry Christmas, Renee. Do you know when Louis is done for the day? Or his schedule for the next few days?"

There was a sound of a mouse click or two, Renee double-checking, because Louis only hired people who double-checked and got things right every time. "He didn't know how long he was going to be out of the office today. He does have marked that he's in Mayville until January second, but I guess that's changed with these emergency meetings."

"No idea who they're with?"

"Sorry. He's got them marked as confidential."

Ronnie lifted her head and pressed it back against the headrest. More secrets. She was getting so tired of those. And as if to emphasize the fact, her phone beeped in her ear. Low battery. Great.

"Okay," Ronnie said. "Can you tell him I called?"

"Sure. How are things out there? Lots of snow?"

"Oh yeah." She started to say something else, and her phone cut off, its battery dead. Probably just as well. Renee was sounding far too wistful for a situation she knew nothing about and Ronnie simply didn't have the energy to either lie or explain.

She sat there for almost a full minute, mulling through all the stupid choices she'd been making recently and what she should do about them. Then she took a deep breath, put the truck back in gear, and headed for her parents' house. She needed to let Alex know, in the barest of outlines, what had happened and why he was not ever to set anything up for her on the relationship front ever again.

She could mess up her own life without any help.

14

ALEX WASN'T AT HOME. Despite the cold weather, Suzie said, he'd apparently arranged with the Stephanopoluses and Stony Phelps to have another game out at Stony's rink. He and Nick had been there for the past hour. Alex, Suzie, and Nick actually had to head back to Fort Cleary tomorrow, so this was one of the hockey-mad father-and-son's last chances before Alex had to get back to work.

Their imminent departure on top of everything else made Ronnie suddenly homesick for family and she gathered up Suzie and her mother and Emma and Emma's boyfriend for a massive cookie-making session in her mother's kitchen.

It was way too crowded and way too much fun. By twenty minutes in, Jeff had on one of Ronnie's mom's frilliest aprons and Ronnie sported a nose and forehead of flour and sparkles, and a mouthful of sweet and crunchy peanut-butter cookie dough.

Ronnie's dad hid in his downstairs study with the door bolted and probably barricaded with his bookshelf of ancient legal tomes, a last shield against such outright insanity

~~~~

Mark found his father where he thought he'd be—Stony's private rink, watching his grandsons having at it with Alex Cleary and his son, Nick, along with Aaron, Chris, Stephano, and Stony.

Mark passed on their enthusiastic invitations to join them and instead stole away his father for a drive to the south end of Mayville where Gold Construction had eight hundred square feet of planning and administration offices with an over-height garage and yard in the back for the company-owned backhoes, dump trucks, and other equipment off Tukamuk Lane.

He brought him into his dad's main office, where Mark had spent way too much of his youth, and spread the binders out on the planning table in the middle of it.

"Pull up a chair, Pop," he said. "I've got some serious stuff to go over with you."

~~~~

As hour two of their massive cookie-making session approached, with a production line well-established now—Ronnie in the direction-and-batter-tasting station at the end of the kitchen table nearest the fridge, Jeff collecting ingredients from various kitchen cupboards for her, Emma doing the important jobs of beating egg whites and creaming butter and sugar, Suzie mixing dry and wet ingredients, and Ronnie's mom doing the actual plopping and shaping of the cookie dough on the baking sheets—there was a sound from the hallway outside the kitchen not unlike what Ronnie imagined would be the sound of a snuffling bear emerging from its post-Christmas hibernation to come out and search for food.

"Cinnamon hearts?" said Ronnie's dad as he poked his long face around the edge of the kitchen door.

"I poured a bowl," Ronnie said with a laugh and held up the little crystal dish she grabbed from the dining room hutch and filled, clickety-click, with a bag of the red candies she'd picked up the day she'd shopped for her mother at the Dover Pantry. She just hadn't felt the need to fill it before today as only she and her dad ate them.

Today she'd needed them.

Apparently so had her dad. He eased his lanky frame into the room, slipped around his wife's clutches while still managing to kiss her cheek, and ended up at Ronnie's side. He popped four of the little hot candies into his mouth and grinned at her as his face became visibly flushed.

Ronnie laughed and allowed herself one more, since her taster duties were at an end. The last batch of cookies, this one banana-nut, chocolate chip, was mixed and fluffy and down the table to Ronnie's mom, who now had help from both Emma and Suzie in plopping tablespoon-sized goops of dough onto the baking sheets.

Suddenly Ronnie's mom stopped what she was doing and looked up, stricken.

"Oh, my goodness," she said.

Suzie leaned over, worried. "What is it, Mom?"

"I completely forgot about lunch."

~~~~

Mark sat tensely in the rolling armchair he'd pulled up to the worktable thirty minutes ago beside his father and spread out his four binders. The first two were everything he'd been able to pull together, in photocopies and executive summary form about the current projects that Gold Construction had recently finished, still had in the works, or had in some stage of a bidding process. It wasn't a pretty picture.

His father finished pushing the second binder away from him and swiveled his armchair towards Mark, making it creak a little as he leaned his compact, round body back in it. "We've had a difficult few years," he said, like he needed to explain.

Mark nodded. "I know. I was there for a bunch of it, remember?"

"But your projections..." His father waved a hand at the last binder he'd read, the last section of it. "Do you really think it's as bad as this? You know about our other contracts— Durham Bridge, the schoolhouse in Cavarry?"

"I'm not saying Gold Construction won't survive, Pop.

You've been through worse. I'm just saying there are some real problems. Probably more tough times ahead unless we try some different things."

He could see his father tense up, even as the old man spread his hands open before him. "That's why you're at Harvard. To make us *nuatare nell'oro.* Swimming in gold, right?"

It totally missed the fact he'd gone to Harvard to get away from GC altogether, but Mark said, "Right, Pop. Or at least staying healthy. Moving into the new world of things."

The tension in his father's body seemed to ratchet up another notch. The old man wasn't stupid. He had to have known when Mark asked for a special meeting like this that it was going to be difficult.

"So do you want me to read through everything you got here"—Mark's father patted the second set of binders—"or do you want to just give it to me straight and quickly?"

"You make it sound like I'm about to hand you a death sentence."

"I see the name of Stanco Brothers in the first pages. After you tell me that our businesses don't fit together and don't have to fit together."

Mark took a deep breath. His father had caught even more than he'd thought. Never had much formal education, was still slow to really use his smartphone to do half the things it could do, but the old man had lived a life of doing deals, watching numbers, managing expenses and contracts, changing building practices, changing financial landscapes.

And he was still here. His company, started as a one-man renovation business, was still here and, if not thriving, still operating, still respected, still doing quality work.

"You *don't* have to fit together, Pop. Gold's not going bankrupt or anything. But it's going to have to shrink and it's going to struggle awhile, be very touch and go, if it keeps going it completely alone. And this thing with Stanco, as long as it's handled right, could be a real opportunity to grow without cutting corners or changing your building style."

"You call them 'slash and burn', this Stanco outfit."

Mark nodded, feeling the ice in his stomach as he remembered Edward Stanco's cold sarcasm on the phone. "Yeah. They do that a lot. But not all the time. Depends whether they're forced to do better. I'm suggesting they value this contract you've got enough, that you can force them to do better."

"Building standards, site practices, environment..." He eyed the proposal binders.

"All that. Remember, I've worked for you for half my life, Pop. I know what you do."

His father looked him in the eye. "I know you know what I do. I just don't know if you can control what *they* do."

Mark forced his face calm to fight the same doubt that came roaring through his own ears like a twelve-alarm fire. "That's what contracts are for. I've drafted up all the standards I think you need to get them to agree to. They'll try to change all of them. You negotiate. And if you have to, you walk away from the deal. Simple."

His father hadn't stopped holding his gaze. "Not so simple."

"Why not?"

"Because they come to me through you. They think this is going to give them some kind of—what do you say?—leverage. They got something on you? You didn't tell me how you know they want to deal. Something going to happen to you if I say no?"

~~~~

"Dad, I need to borrow the truck," Ronnie said as they finished lunch of leftover-Christmas-turkey-and-cranberry-sauce sandwiches, along with butter pickles and a half-dozen other small nibbles that her mother had strewn around the kitchen table to make it feel like a real family meal.

He looked up, his mouth full. Emma took the moment to insert a sly little, "And to where or *whom* might you be driving, Veronica?"

"None of your beeswax, Emmaline." Not her real name, but as traditionally despised between them as Ronnie's own full-sized moniker. "Dad?"

Her father swallowed and nodded, wiping his mouth. "Of course, dear. But if…um…from your sister's subtle question… you are thinking of going to visit Mark, I should tell you that I received an e-mail from Louis just before I came in to join all of you. He's heading back out here first thing tomorrow morning.

Says he has some important news to share with you."

Ronnie blushed so hard her scalp tingled. Did *everyone* know of her interest in Mark Stephanopolus? Clearly they did. Suzie was smiling to herself. Jeff was pointedly not meeting her eyes. Ronnie's mother was studying her face to gauge her reaction, maybe looking for a confirm or deny?

Then the rest of what Ronnie's father had said hit her. "Why wouldn't Louis call or text me directly?"

"Um…" Her mother held up a tentative hand. "He did call earlier this morning, dear. When you were out." Unspoken— *With Mark. Up on the Ridge, where there's crappy cell phone reception.*

And the lack of a call or call to her cell since then? Well, Louis had been in a meeting when Ronnie had tried to call him. Then…oh, good grief. She hadn't recharged her cell. She pulled it out of her pocket, pushed its start button a few times, and stared at its black screen like it had betrayed her. "Great," she said. "Important news. A dead cell phone. A snoopy family. You know what? I'm going to plug this in, then I'm going for a walk."

"You want some company?" Suzie said from across the table.

"Um…no," she snapped, mimicking both her parents. Should have apologized. Stormed out instead.

~~~

175

Mark swiveled back and forth slowly in the GC office armchair, his arms crossed tightly over his chest, as his father read through all his proposals about the GC-Stanco Bros. project partnership a second time. He hadn't told his father about Edward Stanco's threats, of course. This project partnership would only work if his father bought it on the merits. And the merits were *there*.

But outside this office somewhere, in this brilliantly-cold day that seemed to be stretching on forever, was that fiery-haired, emotionally capricious, infinitely exciting and frustrating woman he'd much rather be planning his life with.

She was no doubt at home, having totally written him off now that she'd sampled the goods and found them too difficult or secretive or whatever. Maybe she was already packing her suitcase to head back to Chicago and rejoin Louis, if only to sort out her own feelings in all of this.

Not knowing, while he simultaneously waited for his father's reaction on this Stanco thing, was driving Mark crazy.

He was not good at waiting.

~~~~

"No, Veronica," said the dark-haired woman in the Stephanopolus doorway.

She was far too petite, Ronnie thought as she had at that pre-Christmas dinner, to have delivered the sturdy trio of sons that included Mark. Maybe she was a decoy, somehow designed to keep her and Mark apart. Kind of like Ronnie's father, who *talked* like he was on her side all the time, but then resisted giving her the keys to his truck so that she'd had to stomp out of the house in her boots and walk what felt like miles across the east side of town to get to the Stephanopoluses' house, exact address courtesy of the old-fashioned address book she'd snuck into her father's office to check before leaving.

"No," the dark-haired woman repeated. "He didn't come home since he left this morning to see his father up on the Ridge. I mean…"

Mark's mother looked momentarily confused as she squinted at Ronnie, and Ronnie realized that this woman, too, had somehow known about her and Mark meeting up on the Ridge. Such a well-kept secret, Alex and Stephano. Thanks, guys.

"Well, when you see him…" Ronnie let it die. When she saw him, what? Have him drive around and find Ronnie? To what end? Was he going to tell her something new? Was she going to suddenly decide she wanted to change her whole life for a guy she barely knew, who was keeping some kind of significant secret from her?

"Never mind," she said.

"I tell him you came here."

"No!" Ronnie held up a hand. "I mean, I want to surprise him with something. I'll come by tomorrow. Okay? Don't want to ruin the surprise."

She smiled brightly to reassure Mark's mother, then turned, jammed her gloved hands into her pockets for extra warmth, and set off on a long walk to clear her head.

~~~~

It was almost four by the time Mark got a tentative agreement out of his father to at least meet with Edward Stanco and talk through the possibilities. Then Mark drove his father home and backed right out of the driveway again to go over and see Ronnie.

He couldn't tell her everything, of course, but maybe there was some way he could be honest enough with her to reassure her that he wasn't hiding anything out of guilt or shame. Maybe there *had* been a little of that earlier, but with her, he just couldn't afford it. He needed her too much. It sounded a little crazy to him even now. A lot like how his father had described being hit when he'd met Mark's mother. With a *colpo de fulmine*. A thunderbolt of love.

And maybe Ronnie didn't feel the same way—no, of course she didn't feel the same way or she wouldn't have rabbited out of the work office up on the ridge where they'd lain together—but he had to give her at least enough that she'd give them a chance.

This Chicago vs. Mayville thing? They'd work it out. The thing with Louis? It was so obvious to Mark that Ronnie would emotionally die in that relationship, he couldn't take it seriously. So there was just the secret thing. And for that he just needed time. The proposal he'd put together wouldn't only satisfy his father, but even Ronnie's father. It was about as close to the ideal of steady, careful growth as this town was ever going to see. And when Ronnie saw that…

He reached the Cleary lane and turned in, parked behind the Prius, and jogged up to the front door.

Ronnie's father answered his knock, looking grave. "She's not here," he said. "And no, I'm not going to tell you where she is. Look, boyo, I know my daughter. All bright and sparkly much of the time, but when she gets something in her mind that she really needs to work through, she needs time. You interrupt that and you're just letting yourself in for a whole passel of trouble."

"I get that, sir. I just figured that—"

"I know. Logic and reason. Fact and feelings. But sometimes you just have to let women sort things out on their own and *then* step in. If you catch my meaning."

"I think I do."

"Good."

"And I hope you're right."

"If it's meant to be…"

"Do you really believe in that kind of superstition? Sir?"

Colin Cleary twitched his brows up, then his corners of his mouth twitched up too. "Not in the least. But I do believe the rest of what I'm telling you, boyo. Ronnie's no shrinking violet. Let *her* come to you."

"I'll give her until tomorrow afternoon."

Ronnie's father gave him a little head bow and shut the door.

As Mark walked back to the Super Duty pickup, his cell phone rang. It was the sly, cutting voice of Edward Stanco.

"Just talked to your father, kid. Good work. I'm coming there tomorrow for a meeting."

"You want me in the room?"

"Maybe not for the first go round. Not sure. Be close."

"I'll be here."

"Yes, you will, kid. Yes, you will."

When Mark clicked the hang-up, his stomach was roiling. But whether it was with anticipation about Ronnie, nerves over his father meeting Edward Stanco, or a general sense of something else in the air, he wasn't sure.

15

WHEN RONNIE WOKE ON DECEMBER 28, Christmas already seemed like a long-ago dream. She went to the window of the downstairs guest room where she'd slept and looked out at the sun-sparkled frosty trees and snow that ran around the northeast corner of the house. She thought she heard a car in the distance somewhere, the crack of a snapping tree branch, but everything else was still.

Then, almost on cue, she smelled coffee and heard her mother bustling around in the kitchen. The Cleary household was waking up.

But she didn't want to exit her room yet. She wanted to hang onto this wonderful, sensual dream she'd been having about finding her perfect place in life, where she was adored and protected, held and valued, and...

Oh my goodness. Not really a dream at all. More a memory. It was what she'd felt up at that makeshift office on Putter's Ridge, being held and kissed and stroked by Mark as he said all the right things, made her feel like she was talented and doing the right things with her life.

She touched her lips and felt the smile there. Added a sense of wonder to it.

How could she have run out on him up there? For Louis? Because Mark wouldn't immediately answer all her questions about his plans for her father's business? It had seemed so critical at the time. Enough to send her on a two hour-plus solo walk around the town in the snow. Enough to keep her quiet and surly all through dinner when she'd finally come back here. Enough to make her go to bed early because she couldn't stand being around people, including herself.

And then, overnight, through her dreams, she seemed to have worked it all out. Like she'd just had to process everything for it all to fall into place and make sense. Perspective. Through Mark's eyes, the course of her life seemed to make sense. There were still things to work out, of course, but he somehow gave her the sense that it would all be okay. Better than okay.

If only she could work out the issues between them personally. Because she didn't want to lose him, she realized. She needed to tell him that. Then she needed to make him talk. And she needed to figure out just how they could handle the practicalities of their small-town vs. big-city relationship divide.

"Where there's a will…" she whispered to herself, then bounced from the window to grab her robe and join her mother in the kitchen to help make breakfast.

~~~~

"That Cleary girl come by here yesterday," Mark's mother said as Mark slathered a healthy layer of peanut butter onto the French toast he'd made for himself. The more European *collazione* of a latte with rolls and jam that his mother prepared for the others had never been quite enough for him.

He froze and looked up. "Which Cleary girl?"

"You know. Red hair."

"Ronnie."

"Ve-*ron*-eeca! Yes!"

She said it like it was a surprise, but she'd never been a great actress. Her behavior before he'd gone up to Putter's Ridge yesterday morning, her concerned look when she'd asked him about that little visit last night, even her little fake "remembering" of Ronnie's name this morning told him she was well aware of his interest in Ronnie Cleary. And maybe aware, too, that his time with her yesterday hadn't gone well. (Though actually it *had*, at first. It had been like a trip to Heaven then to Hell in two quick hours. A throwback to his swimming classes with her as a kid.)

"Why didn't you tell me that last night, Mom?" Maybe before he drove all over Mayville looking for her after her father said she was out?

"She said I should no tell. She said she has surprise she gonna deliver to you today."

Stephano, who'd just come downstairs and entered the kitchen, said, "Who's coming by with what?"

"Veronica Cleary," their mother said, almost singing the name. "She is coming with a surprise for Marcario!"

"Whew-hoo!" Stephano said, going to the espresso machine by the sink to make himself a cup. "Maybe it's an engagement ring, Marky. You think?"

"No," said their mother. "That no proper a thing for a girl to do."

"Twenty-first century, Mom. These days the girls take control, right, bro?"

Mark felt like he should be jumping on Stephano and slapping him down, but he was frankly too hungry and involved in slicing up the bananas to top his French toast with peanut butter. And tingling nervously with his own speculations about what Ronnie intended to do. He just hoped it came before Edward Stanco arrived in town around noon. Because after that time, his ability to juggle emotional powder kegs was going to be fully taxed with just his dad and his possible future boss.

"I think that whatever Ronnie chooses to give me won't be half of what she gave me yesterday," he said blithely and walked his emptied banana peel over to the below-sink compost bucket.

That shut them up. He was amused to see his mother's dusky face going a deeper shade of rose while his baby brother's lower jaw literally hung open. Then the kid sputtered, leaned back against the counter by the now-creaking espresso machine, pressure building, and grinned.

"You're welcome," he said.

"Outcome still uncertain," Mark said as he poured some table syrup over his breakfast creation and began eating.

"Isn't it always?"

The exchange ended as a tumult at the front door announced the arrival of the two elder brothers and their families for breakfast.

~~~~

Everyone had finished eating breakfast at the Clearys by 10:00 and Alex and family were doing their final packing to head out.

Ronnie was filled with bittersweet emotions as she helped her mother clean, then paced around the house, supposedly looking for things Nick or Alex or Suzie might have left hiding under a couch or something.

She desperately wanted her brother and his family to finish packing and go already so she could head out to find Mark. At the same time, Alex leaving felt like the disappearance of her strongest ally in this surprising new development in her love life. Her love life? No, her whole life in general, given how it promised to reshape everything she'd imagined for her future.

Ronnie's dad, always her stalwart supporter and the first person she'd normally turn to in this kind of life-defining day, felt sadly unavailable to her because of his stupid running-for-town-council thing. She hadn't revealed to him her suspicions about Mark being maybe caught up in something that was going to clash with his politics. She didn't want to risk it. It was yet another reason why she paced, the calm decision of her early morning replaced by a sense of building uncertainty and nerves.

It wasn't until nearly eleven that Alex and family were finally ready to head out. By then Ronnie had actually started gnawing on her fingernails.

The goodbyes themselves, accompanied as they always were by endless posings for photographs of the entire clan—Ronnie's father had finally purchased himself a good tripod so he could get himself in the pictures—took a good twenty minutes. By the end of it, Ronnie felt like yelling, *Just GO!*

Then they finally did and Ronnie felt like crying.

It passed. She wanted to get over to the Stephanopolus home and get her life sorted out. And if her father, who was deep in a discussion with Ronnie's mother in the kitchen, didn't loan her the pickup right this minute, she'd just walk! It was only about twenty or thirty blocks. She'd done it yesterday. She could do it again today. She couldn't believe, actually, how rarely people in this town walked anywhere. Back in Chicago she walked everywhere.

But even as she went back to the front entry hall to get her heavy cloth coat and just go, her father trailed after her with the pickup's key ring whirling around his index finger. "I'm heading over to the Gold Construction office downtown to talk with Andreas about something," he said. "Mom suggested you might like to come along. Mark is apparently there this morning."

The office downtown? Ronnie realized, abashed, that she didn't even know where that was. And that if she'd walked all the way over to the Stephanopolus home, she would have once more found Mark missing. She also would have appeared pretty clueless for not calling ahead, like her father had obviously done, to find out where the person she wanted to visit actually was.

So she agreed, got on her boots and coat, and joined her dad in the truck. They drove south down Duck and then west on Glenn all the way in to Main Street. As her father turned south there and did the slow stop-and-go heading south, her father pointed out all the changes that had been going on in Mayville. He seemed to know not only every shop owner, but their families, their histories, their aspirations.

"Forget running for the town council, Dad," Ronnie said. "You should be mayor."

"In a few years, maybe," he said and gave her a lopsided grin. Then he grew serious again. "A lot depends on what happens next with the town. We're at a bit of a crossroad."

Ronnie felt her insides tighten. "The development thing? Woodwand?"

"It's what I'm going to see Andreas about right now. A little bird tweeted to me that he's got a major meeting going on today, right now, that could have a serious impact on that."

"With who?"

"Whom."

"Yeah. And I'm guessing from your frown it's someone you don't like."

He grunted in response and pursed his lips.

"Someone you've dealt with before?"

Her father pursed his lips tighter.

"When you were part of the Mayville's Future thing?" The story of that had come out at yesterday's cookie-making session. How the current town council had decided they needed a grand vision for the future of their town and had set up a series of meetings for input from the town residents. Ronnie's dad had taken part. His disgust with what he called a short-sighted fiscal desperation had been what made him decide to run for council member in the upcoming elections.

"One of the proposals the town council floated at that fiasco was by the Stanco Brothers, out of Boston, for Pete's sake."

"The ones that—"

"The ones your two suitors were arguing about over dinner at our house last week. Yes. I kept my mouth shut out of respect for your boyfriend, fiancé… Which is it, by the way? Your mother thinks you've been getting sweet on Andreas's son, Mark, which kind of complicates things, doesn't it?"

"You're deflecting, Dad."

Her father huffed and leaned farther over the steering wheel, gripping it tightly as they stopped at the last stop light going south. "The younger of the two Stanco brothers actually came out to the Mayville's Future second meeting and laid out what he wanted to do with Mayville. Most of the people who were at that meeting wisely booed him down and just about rode him out of town on a rail. He actually had the nerve to call Mayville a relic, a deadwater little spot on the map that, like way too many towns in the Midwest, was going to just shrivel up and die if it didn't accept his vision of massive growth and commercialization. I personally wanted to slug him in his weasely, East Coast face."

"But how do you really feel about him?"

He missed the humor in her question and barreled on—the light changed and he lurched the pickup forward—about the profit-driven culture of Stanco Brothers and their ilk, gaining a bigger head of steam than Ronnie had seen in him in decades. The last time she'd seen him this worked up, in fact, had been that trial a decade ago, when he'd been defending a man of Persian descent who'd been almost tarred and feathered by some locals who claimed to have heard him discussing a terrorist plot on the phone with some other "foreigners." That had been her father's libertarian side. This current issue obviously tweaked his more conservative, yet anti-big-business, roots.

Men were a mystery, no doubt about it.

Main Street ended in a little J-curve and turned into Tukamuk Lane, which was an interesting collection of low-end bungalows and sprawling businesses, one of them being Gold Construction.

As Ronnie's father pulled into the parking area in front of the GC building's solid, unpretentious front door, he muttered a little curse under his breath. Ronnie followed his gaze and saw Andreas Stephanopolus coming around the west side of the building, walking side-by-side with a skeletal, vulpine-looking man in a calf-length, black overcoat that almost gleamed in the grayish sunlight. Probably fine merino wool. The man was looking down, listening seriously to whatever it was that Andreas was saying. From her father's reaction, Ronnie guessed that this man had to be the younger of the Stanco brothers.

At their heels, with his hands stuffed into his workman's parka, his head also down, walked Mark.

"Why is Andreas even *talking* with him?" Ronnie's father said.

But Ronnie didn't wonder. From Mark's presence here, the way he was walking, the fact he'd been at Harvard, which was in Boston, wasn't it? Where her father had said the Stanco Brothers were based. And Mark had said he'd met the brothers personally. Put that together with Mark keeping some kind of secret from her and it all seemed to make a sick kind of sense. Despite his denunciation of them at that pre-Christmas dinner, Mark had brought the Stancos back to Mayville to meet his father.

Then, as Ronnie followed her father's lead and climbed out of the pickup, she felt another one-two punch of dread.

There in the same parking lot that they'd driven into, but

off to the left side so that she hadn't seen it while she'd been sitting in the truck, sat a tan-colored Range Rover, just like the one Louis had borrowed from his friend to drive to Mayville in last week's snowstorm.

It could have been a coincidence, but with Louis due back in Mayville today, Ronnie doubted it.

And she got her second punch of dread as she saw who was appearing around the corner of the building following Mark. As she'd half-expected. Louis. Dressed in the same kind of vulpine, merino-wool overcoat that Stanco wore. A huge, box-like, black legal briefcase hung from one of his hands and, as Ronnie watched, he shifted its obvious weight to his other hand. Louis saw her standing beside her father's truck and burst into such a look of intense self-satisfaction that Ronnie thought she might be sick right there, all over the salted snow and ice of the parking lot.

Maybe the shift in Louis's focus was felt by Mark because he looked up just a beat later, saw Ronnie, and gave a weak smile and wave. Andreas, too, looked over, and, finally, the man who had to be Stanco.

The two older men paused just outside the front door of the Gold Constructions offices and waited as Ronnie's father stormed over to them. Ronnie, gut in knots, strode after him.

"Andreas!" Ronnie's father said as he reached them. "What are you doing here?"

The head of the Stephanopolus clan sighed as he met the assault. His eyes looked tired, with heavy bags under them, an effect on his face that made them seem like mined-out pits at the end of the earth. "We're talking. At this point that is all we are doing."

"Talking about what?"

The bony-thin man whom Ronnie took to be Stanco, looked up at Ronnie's father with a bemused smirk. "You're entitled to know everyone's business in town, Mr. Cleary? My understanding is that you haven't even run for public office yet. Not that public office would give you any special right to know what two businessmen are talking about."

"We might be working together," Andreas said, stating the obvious. But the direct contradiction of Stanco's assertion of privacy made that man's smirk twitch downwards.

"But *why?*" Ronnie's father pressed.

Andreas raised his chest, looked at Ronnie's father, at Stanco, glanced quickly at his son, and said, "It is a business discussion. That is all I wish to say for now."

"Andreas…"

"No! Colin, you are a friend and someone I respect. But this is not your place! Go home. Take your daughter and go home!"

From a foot behind him, Ronnie could feel her father's body vibrate from the verbal slap. He strained forward almost like he wanted to grapple with Andreas, or maybe attack Stanco, and Ronnie had a quick flash of where she might have gotten her own impulsiveness from. But her father managed to rein himself in at last and settled back on his heels.

"Just...don't make any rash decisions, Andreas," he said. "I'd hate to be on opposite sides of the table when you go to Council for approvals."

Andreas said nothing, though his eyes seemed to be carrying the weight of the world. He finally turned towards the front door of the Gold Construction offices, opened it, and gestured for his guest to enter. Stanco waved Mark in first but shook his head at Louis. He took Louis's heavy briefcase from him, then entered behind with Andreas and Mark. The door closed behind the three of them.

Louis, his smug façade only shaken for a moment, turned back towards Ronnie and her father.

"Mr. Cleary," he said with a nod of his head. "Ronnie. Lovely day, isn't it?"

Ronnie felt her father tensing up again and stepped forward before he could say or do something that he'd regret later. Louis seemed to bring that out in people. "Louis," she said. "Let's go for a drive."

~~~~

Inside the GC offices, Mark felt like growling every bit as much as it had looked like Ronnie's father wanted to. This meeting was *not* going as planned.

The first sign, of course, had been the appearance of Louis, arriving in his borrowed Land Rover with its posh leather seats, as Edward Stanco's personal chauffeur. It made

Mark feel immediately stupid. Worse, it made him look stupid or worse in the eyes of his father. That he hadn't known of the involvement of Ronnie's boyfriend in this deal was reprehensible. From Mark's father's point of view, it showed Mark to be either out of the loop, or withholding information. Pulling a fast one.

Mark had muttered his ignorance of Louis's involvement when the two out-of-towners had shown up, but the look his father had given him had held such levels of disappointment that Mark literally felt himself shrink down in his bones. Even so, his father had insisted Mark stick by his side, regardless of what Stanco wanted.

Which meant Mark had been with them on the tour through the Gold Construction equipment storage yards. Of course GC only kept the basics that were adequate for smaller jobs here. Larger graders and trucks were rented or leased for projects as needed. Edward Stanco probably knew this, but he still managed to oh-so-innocently express his shock at the tiny capital equipment with which Gold Construction operated.

Not only small equipment, he somehow managed to indicate, but outdated as well. Underpowered. He slipped in a backhanded compliment about how wonderful it was that GC managed to do as well as they did with this sort of infrastructure. Edward Stanco apparently couldn't help himself.

And Mark's father just took it. He nodded, blank-faced, at each barbed question, each unasked for business assessment.

Only because Mark knew him so well, could Mark see the hollowing out of his father's face, like any hope he'd had to make this an uplifting move forward was being scooped away, one acid-dipped word at a time.

Which let Mark finally understand that this game was being played with rules he didn't yet understand. In Mark's mind, Mark's father held all the cards. He had Mark's proposals. He had a major company with major resources coming to him, hat in hand, ready to give GC the capital it needed *if* they could reach an agreement as to terms. Or GC could just say no and that was it. Mark's future job with Stanco Brothers would be gone, but he'd have at least held up his end of the bargain Stanco had said they'd made. Nor harm, no foul.

Now, though, Mark realized that Stanco just getting in the door to meet with his father was the Stanco victory, the breaching of the castle gates. It was written in every move Stanco made, every slump of Mark's father's shoulders.

Which Mark still didn't understand. But he felt it. He knew. He just didn't understand why. So, as Edward Stanco and Mark's father sat down at the same table where Mark had spread out the binders only yesterday, Mark pulled his chair in close beside his father to listen closely to both what was said and not said.

Stanco opened the discussions. "I read through your proposals," he said, indicating the heavy briefcase on the floor. Indicating also that Mark's father had, unbeknownst to Mark, scanned and sent the entire set of proposals to Stanco yesterday after seeing Mark. More technology comfort there than Mark had seen his father usually display.

Even more disconcerting was that Stanco had apparently read and digested everything in one afternoon, then he'd flown to Chicago (or already been there?), met with Louis, and driven out here the very next morning.

Either Stanco was eager, or superhumanly sharp and efficient, or both.

"Yes," said Mark's father, like he'd expected nothing less of the man.

"You know there's a reason why Stanco Brothers was one of the few international building firms to sail through the recession and emerge with even more market share. We deal in reality. We sell dreams, but behind the sales pitch, we work with realistic budgets and cost projections. There's very little in these proposals that will let us do that."

Mark's father didn't sigh, didn't raise up his chest like he had to Ronnie's father outside. He just looked Stanco in the eye and said flatly, "We follow all these rules at Gold Construction. We manage."

Stanco smiled. Mark wondered how he could have ever seen that smile as anything but the shark smile it was. It was subtler than Louis Beauchamp's smirk, but probably only because Edward Stanco had had longer to polish it.

"About how well Gold Construction is managing," he said. "I've seen a complete breakdown of your company's financials…"

Mark, his face getting hot, gave his father a subtle head shake to tell him that he'd had nothing to do with that, but his father wasn't even looking at him. He was just staring, dead-eyed, at Edward Stanco, as the Bostoner ran through the sorry state of Gold Construction and its prospects for the future.

Yet even that shouldn't have accounted for Mark's father's state. Because Mark's father knew all this. Mark had gone over it with him yesterday, including the assurance that they could still proceed without Stanco. It would just be difficult.

No, Mark's father saw further in this game than Mark did. Somehow Mark had missed something critical.

He leaned forward, frowning intently, trying to pick up what it was.

~~~~

"So how long have you been working with the Stanco Brothers?" Ronnie asked Louis as they drove back onto Main.

As she spoke, she watched her father, ahead of them, weave his Toyota pickup erratically through the sparse traffic like he couldn't get away from the Gold Construction offices fast enough. The sight made Ronnie suddenly uncomfortable that she was riding in a vehicle that probably cost three times what her father's truck cost. It even smelled rich, like Louis had stuck some kind of delicate lemony scent release into one of the air vents. Its engine purred. The usual crunch of snow and ice under the tires was just a dull rumble in the Range Rover.

She fingered the smooth leather of her passenger seat and turned her head to look directly at Louis. "Well?"

"How long have *I* been working with the Stancos?" Louis said. "Maybe you should be asking yourself how long *Mark* has been working with them."

"What do you mean?"

"You think his dad wanted to meet with Edward Stanco? No. He only did it because Mark persuaded him. Because Mark and Mr. Stanco started planning how Stanco Brothers was going to get into Mayville months ago. That was Mark's mission in coming back here."

Ronnie felt a heavy weight pressing down on her chest. "That's a lie."

Louis laughed. "Ask him. You know, it frankly surprised me, too. I only found out yesterday. Guy's a good actor, what with that whole speech about how his dad's company is nothing like the Stancos and Panderos Homes builders of the world. And here he was just buttering up his old man the whole time. Not to mention your father and his family."

"What do you mean?"

"You think he didn't know about your dad running for Town Council? How influential he is? You think the way he gave that little tour of his dad's project up on Putter's Ridge wasn't laying the groundwork to win over his council vote?"

"No. Not true." And on that point, she was sure she was right. She remembered the stricken look on Mark's face when Ronnie's father had mentioned his political plans. Of course, the stricken look *did* fit with him already being caught up with the Stancos at that point. And with him wanting to talk with her that day?

"Okay, maybe he didn't know about your dad's politics," Louis conceded, reading her face. "But I bet the Stancos still told him to play nice with him because *they* knew. Might have even suggested he get close to Colin Cleary's daughter."

"No."

"No?"

"That's low, Louis. You feel threatened and you start making things up."

"Am I? I'm guessing at some things, but not about Mark working for Edward Stanco. You ask him directly. I'm sure he'll justify it ten ways to Sunday. Maybe say he's here to help his dad. Worried about the old man's health. Whatever. Then ask him what Mr. Stanco promised him if he came through for them. What he'd get if he delivered Gold Construction, and, incidentally, the future development of Mayville, to Stanco Brothers on a platter."

Ronnie stared out the window at all the old familiar storefronts from her childhood flashing by. A few new ones too, but not enough to change the sense of *home* that still hung around this place. Didn't Mark feel that? He was the one actually coming back here to live, while she was the one trying to stay away.

Or—the dark thought just crept in quietly from the side of her mind as they approached the north end of town and

Louis swung them right onto a side road, heading east—was Mark's mind even more devious than Louis was suggesting? Mark had said he really wanted to be in Boston, or New York, or Chicago. Anywhere but small-town Mayville. He said he'd gone to Harvard as much for the different mindset as anything. He'd even talked about being "trapped" here because of his father's condition.

Maybe that was all true and his working with Stanco was a sick kind of revenge. If he had to live in Mayville, either for his father's health or for whatever reward the Stancos had promised him, then maybe he'd strike right at the conservative core of the place, make it so it *wasn't* so small town anymore. Or just so it wasn't the same. If he couldn't have the career he wanted, then maybe the people here who were stopping him shouldn't have the town they wanted.

"How long do you think they'll be talking?" Ronnie asked Louis without looking at him.

"A few hours, I would guess. Maybe longer. It'll take that long to iron out a preliminary agreement on how Stanco Brothers and Gold Construction are going to work together on the Putter's Ridge project and beyond."

"Unless Andreas turns Stanco down."

"He won't. You know how I know? He brought me down with him. And my time's expensive. Mr. Stanco would only have shelled out for me if he knew I'd be drawing up paperwork on this trip."

Somehow they'd made it to Duck Road and Louis turned

them north towards Ronnie's parents' house and slowed to a crawl like a teenage boy reluctant to end a date.

Ronnie turned and looked at him. "So you think Stanco will bend enough that Andreas will be satisfied they can really work together? Or what? He's going to offer him so much money that Andreas just can't refuse?"

Louis smirked. "He'll do something for sure. I've worked with him on two other deals, and I can tell you he always has incredible intel about his negotiating opponents. In this case I assume he got his intel from Mark. He'll use it somehow. He'll get the deal he wants."

The crushing weight on Ronnie's chest had grown so great she could barely breathe. As Louis prepared to turn into the driveway to the Cleary family home, she shook her head and pointed him to keep driving. To the end of Duck. Left to Circle Road. She didn't know to where, not to Putter's Ridge, not back to Chicago, not yet, just not back under her father's gaze.

Louis quietly took the route she pointed him on. As they drove, Ronnie leaned her forehead against the cold window and stared out at the snowy fields whipping by.

Oh, Mark, she sent out through the cold. *What have you done?*

16

FOR MOST OF THE LAST HOUR, Mark had felt like an inconvenient bystander watching two business heavyweights slugging it out. Then Edward Stanco began talking about what Stanco Brothers would be bringing to the table and turned to Mark.

"Run down Woodwand International for your father, would you, Mark?"

Mark almost fell off his chair.

"He's told me about this Woodwand already," Mark's father said.

"What did he tell you?"

"Who they are. That they are going to come here, maybe, to Mayville. But maybe only if you are working with us to ensure there will be enough homes for them."

Mark stared at his father. He'd never said anything about Woodwand's setting up here as being conditional on a GC-Stanco Brothers deal. Though the obviousness of it now hit him in the face. It was a bargaining chip for the Stancos—a club that Edward had used to bully Mark into compliance, and no doubt a sweetener for the deal the man wanted to do now with Mark's father.

"Good. Good." Stanco eyed Mark with what might have been a newfound respect. "Then you've got a pretty good idea of the sort of leverage we can bring to the table beyond just capital and experience with bigger projects."

"And what are you going to give my son if I go along with this?" Mark's father said.

Mark felt something cold and hard sink to the pit of his stomach, but Edward Stanco didn't even skip a beat.

"He'd help coordinate this project, of course. He'd either work directly with you or be the general project manager. Keep up your legendary quality that way, right?"

"And after this project?" Mark's father said. He didn't look at his son.

"Stanco Brothers has a lot of projects going on around the country. I've offered to bring him into the loop on those, at a project management level to begin with, but with the opportunity to move up the management ranks as he proves himself."

"All over the country."

"All over." Stanco affirmed. "It's a good thing, don't you think, when a father can give his son the kind of boost into a major career that you've given yours. With Harvard, I mean. With all the experience he's had with you. And now this. It's the kind of advancement every self-made man wishes for his family. If I'd had a son—that unfortunately was not in the cards for my wife and I—it's the sort of thing I'd do. Not to put too fine a point on it, Andreas, but I'd like to treat Marcario here like the son I never had. You've helped him up this far. I'd like to help him the rest of the way."

Mark felt like throwing up. He made himself sit up tall in his chair and tried to catch his father's eye, but Andreas Stephanopolus, always so full of life and connected to the people around him, especially his family, seemed lost in another world. His eyes stared through the table top. His face sagged, slack-jawed and ashen. For a moment Mark worried he'd been pushed too far, that he might have another heart attack.

While Edward Stanco sat back in his swivel chair in the studied posture of someone at their ease, simply waiting for his negotiating partner to consider what had been offered.

Except that Mark didn't buy it. He might not have seen far enough into this game to see how his father would have figured out Stanco had made Mark an offer, but he did understand men like Stanco. At least a little. He could smell the sweaty eagerness underneath the man's placid smile. He could also see the clicking in the eyes, the calculating brain. Playing on the classic immigrant aspirations of Mark's father. Had Stanco been counting on that way back when he made the offer to Mark? Probably. Playing both on Mark's needs *and* the needs of his father in one easy little ploy.

Uh-unh. That wasn't right.

"Actually," Mark said and had to clear a frog out of his

throat, he'd spoken so little in the last hour. "Actually, after considering that offer you made, Edward, I don't think I'll be taking that offer in any case."

Mark's father actually blinked, the first sign of life he'd seen from him in a while.

"What?" Stanco said, filling the word with a world of threat.

"Sorry," Mark said, drawing himself up and, surprisingly finding the ball of nausea in his stomach dissolving away with every breath. It was like committing to that first dive off a dock on a summer day when you knew the water was freezing but you'd just have to manage it. Or, ironically, saying yes to a job you weren't sure you could manage. Or reaching out to kiss Ronnie when, hell, it threatened to send everything he knew about everything into a maelstrom of chaos.

"It just strikes me," he said, looking earnestly at Stanco so the man could see there was absolutely no prevarication in him; it wasn't his way, "that my working with you, during the project or afterwards, is not what this negotiation should be about. Nor is it what we talked about when I first met you. You wanted me to see if there was a solid way your company and my dad's company could work together. That's all. That's what I agreed to. And we're not even going to talk about all the other things you tried to ladle onto that agreement."

Mark stood up, subtly emphasizing his solid health, strength, and youth that easily outdid that of either of the other two men in the room. "I found you a way that I think

Stanco Brothers and Gold Construction could work together. It's right there." He pointed at the open binders on the table. "And contrary to your assertions about the real world of business and what it takes to succeed, it's a solid plan and I think you know it. You may not want to bend your normal business practices to make it work, and that's your prerogative. Just don't use me as a lever."

Both men were looking at him now. His father actually had some color in his face again and his eyes sparkled. Stanco's eyes were narrowed.

"You sure you want to do this, kid?" the Boston man said.

Mark's father's head twitched towards Stanco. "'Kid?' That's what you call my son?"

"Term of affection," Stanco muttered.

"No," Mark's father said. "I don't think it is. I think it is an insult. Like I think much of this discussion today has been. You, insulting us."

"Andreas..."

"Using my son... Did you get your information about Gold Construction's financials from him?"

Stanco snorted. "Would have taken it if he'd offered, but he's almost as stubborn as his father, I'm learning. Other people who work for you are much more open to sharing when they're given the right incentive."

"Bribes..."

"Cash incentives. They understand how real business is done."

Mark's father snorted. "How real business is done by people like you. Yes."

"That's right," Stanco said. "By people who want to build more than a couple of homes in a small town and scrape along wondering how they're going to pay off all their tradesmen and suppliers. Now do you want to step out of the scraping-along group and learn how you can actually make money in this noble business we've both chosen? Put the other stuff behind us. It doesn't matter. Just look hard at what we've talked about. Working together, we can do some good houses and make a decent profit here. And if it goes well, I'm not going to hold Mark's flip-flopping against him. There are lots of future projects we could possibly cooperate on."

"Meaning Lonsdon," Mark said, rejoining the conversation. "You're backing the bidder competing with Gold for their new library and fire hall, aren't you?"

Stanco inclined his head, not answering directly. He didn't need to. Mark was finally getting just how much Stanco Brothers wanted to expand through this part of the Midwest and how they'd use almost any tactics to do so.

Mark shook his head slowly. He hadn't sat down and so still towered over two seated men. "You know, if Panderos Homes and the other big construction companies all feel compelled to cut corners and bully their way into contracts like Stanco Brothers does, I'm thinking that the only ray of hope for the future of construction in America must lie with the smaller companies like Gold."

It was like all the air whooshed out of the room. Without moving to stand up or look at Mark at all, Edward Stanco muttered, "That's going to cost you, kid."

Then he pulled out a legal project partnership agreement from among the binders and folders in his box-like briefcase. He slapped it onto the table in front of Mark's father.

"This is the agreement that will get us working together, Andreas. I want you to read it through. It cuts out most of the bullshit quality, environment, and employment things your boy put in his draft but is absolutely fair in its cost and profit sharing between our companies. Minor things, like starting and completion dates, equipment requirements, stuff like that, can be modified right now, this afternoon. It's why I brought Louis Beauchamps with me. He can be a little insufferable at times, but he knows his stuff. He's a good lawyer."

The slight smile Mark had been pleased to see on his father's face faded now and he looked Stanco dead in the eye. "And if I do not sign this?"

Stanco met his gaze with an almost bemused look. "I think you already know. What we *could* do is underbid you on every project you're bidding on now and every one you ever bid on in the future. We could spread rumors about your business practices, smear your son's name. We could alert inspectors to possible shortcomings in recent projects and in the one you're currently doing on Putter's Ridge. And of course the banks could find out just what a bad risk you are so your funding dries up. They might even call in your current loans. We could basically run you into the ground."

Stanco smiled magnanimously. "We're not going to do that, though, because it's a hell of a lot of work and kind of unsavory. No, all we'd need to do here is just block your Lonsdon project and the one you're bidding on in Abbottsford. That and make sure companies like Woodwand know that when they approach the Mayville town council, offering critical development money, it will be with the understanding they'll work with anyone *other* than Gold Construction."

He casually glanced at the Gold Construction financials he'd revealed earlier just to make it clear how Gold wasn't going to make it with their future revenue cut off.

"One way or another, Andreas," he said, "the Stancos always get what we want."

Then he waited.

~~~~

Ronnie studied Louis's half-frozen smirk now and wondered how she could have ever imagined marrying him.

They were back in the Gold Construction parking lot because Louis said he had to stay close. Now, as he stood immediately beside her in the cold, dressed up in his slick lawyer suit under a rich navy-blue merino wool overcoat, contrasting scarf, calf-skin leather gloves, he smelled of money and power. Literally, she realized. She could just pick out his usual spicy, lemony-apple Eros now through his layers of scarf and the parking lot's chill. (It had been *him* she'd smelled in the Land Rover, she realized, not the car itself.) Ronnie's father, by contrast, had always worn simpler, woodsy, pine scents if he wore scents at all. And Mark? She could remember, all of a sudden, his smell of apple soap and musk. Of wanting to lick his skin. Devour him.

She shuddered out a frosty breath. That was probably gone now, her time with Mark. He'd obviously been seduced by all the power she'd once so admired in Louis and now found…deceitful. Had Mark really just gotten close to her to help him in his quest to sell Mayville's future development to Stanco Brothers?

"You're upset," Louis said, going serious. "I'm sorry."

"For what? Telling me the truth? It is the truth, right? Mark's connection to the Stancos. This whole bit about him scouting ways to bring them into Mayville?"

Louis held up his right hand like he was swearing on a bible. "Truth. But I could have let you find out from him."

"No…no…"

"Instead of taking delight in sticking it to him. You know why it gave me pleasure, don't you?"

"Because he's your enemy? He embarrassed you? He went after your girl?"

Louis actually looked rueful. "Guilty on all counts. But there's more than that."

"What?"

"The real reason I enjoyed it was because it let me wake

you up without having to get into the murkiness of what's really going on here."

Ronnie frowned at him. "What do you mean?"

"With you and me? You and him? It seems so…I don't know…pseudo-psyche-Freudy, you know?"

Ronnie felt the slow-burning rage she'd been slowly banking in her gut against Louis from the time she confirmed he was cheating on her, flare up higher in her so she actually tasted the bitter burn of it in the back of her throat. This was his arrogance again. Knowing so much more than her about the real world, real life. As if his extra four years of living, added to his natural genius, put him in a position to understand and judge her every motivation better than she could herself.

"Explain what you mean, Louis. In simple words so that even a university dropout can understand what you mean."

He looked honestly mortified. "I'm so sorry, Ronnie. There I go again, don't I? Doing my pretentious shtick."

She bit her lips. What *was* this? Like the crying in front of her a few nights ago when he arrived, Ronnie just couldn't wrap her head around Louis learning how to be vulnerable and honest.

"It's just…" He stopped and slapped his gloved hands together like they were cold, but she knew they weren't cold. He was finding words. Honesty was *difficult*, wasn't it?

She waited.

"Ronnie…I know I can never apologize enough for the way I treated you in the weeks before you left me in Chicago.

The way I cheated on you, but even worse, the way I thought about you that made me almost *have* to cheat." He quickly held up his hand. "No. Wait. That's wrong. I didn't have to cheat. That's a cop out."

He looked away, still struggling. "The thing is, I was playing, all those weekends we had together, then the times we talked about you moving in with me, with the idea of what it would be like to spend the rest of my life with you. Not just to have you around as some kind of business asset, you understand, but to have as a second part of me. As the woman I shared my thoughts, my feelings, my experience of life with. It scared the hell out of me."

He shrugged, looking down. "My way of dealing with that fear was going and having an affair."

He looked up and met her eyes. "I guess it shouldn't have surprised me that your way of dealing with it was running back to your roots and falling for someone like your father."

Boom. Like a punch in the chest. Ronnie reeled back, almost stumbling. "Like my *father?*"

"I know. Sorry. I'm not implying… But it's someone who celebrates the small town, right? At least on the surface. Comes from a loving family. His father lives here too. He's probably tried to convince you that you could start up your business here, hasn't he? Made it sound like that's what *he* wanted too?"

He'd been losing her on the small town bit because of Mark's speech of wanting to work in Boston or even New

York. And yet, right up until Mark had revealed himself to be in league with the Stancos, she *had* believed him to be a small town boy at heart. How had he done that? He'd been willing to root himself here to look after his ailing father's business. There was that. And it had touched her. That kind of self-sacrificing emotional generosity *was* just like her father's.

Then the conversation she and Mark had had up in the worksite office on Putter's Ridge came back to her. The conversation where he'd made her believe in herself and her talent, just like her father had done all through her childhood. And then Mark, later, angry at her, in almost a throw-away suggestion that she realized now was not a throwaway at all, had suggested Ronnie could take that talent and set up her own shop…right here…in Mayville.

Oh God.

She met Louis's steady gaze and wondered if maybe this pompous Chicago lawyer she'd been ready to tie her life to scant weeks before might actually know her better than anyone else in the world after all.

"Louis…"

Almost without thinking, she found herself stepping into his arms, shaking apart inside, her knees wobbling under her.

Then Louis's arms were around her, strong as she'd always remembered them to be. Not the welcoming, melting into each other kind of strong that she'd had with Mark, but maybe that was for the better. These were arms that let her know who Louis was and who Ronnie was. Each of them would be their true selves with the other, strong and independent, but… honest with each other. A team. And she'd have the life of upward Chicago mobility that she'd seen herself having from the time Louis had swept her off her feet at that charity gala she'd been helping Rolf and Chester cater.

"Hey," he said softly into her hair. Then he pulled her gently back from him and ran a gloved finger under her left eye, bringing it away wet. "Wow, Ron. I don't know that I've ever seen you cry. I've see you get angry, furious even, and confused and even sad, but I didn't think you did tears."

"Really?" Ronnie had trouble believing it. The way her heart felt right now, it was like a river of tears was rushing through her just under her skin. And why? *Why?* Why did it feel like she was losing everything. Because she wasn't. She was just seeing things clearly at last. Where she had to live. Whom she had to live with. Her whole future life.

She forced herself to steady and stepped back holding out her hands, glad she wore gloves because she was sure her hands were corpselike. "Louis, will you drive me home now? And by that, I mean all the way home to Chicago."

He wrinkled up his nose. "You know, I'd love to, Ron, but I have to stay here for Mr. Stanco. Once he and your would-be hometown boy work out a deal, I'm to help them modify and execute the written agreement."

On "would-be hometown boy", Ronnie's found her gaze drawn violently to the front door of the Gold Construction offices, like her body was demanding something stupid. A run at the door. A track-down of Mark, his father, Mr. Stanco.

"You know what I can do, though?" said Louis quickly. "I'll call your dad to come back and get you. And just as soon as everything's wrapped up here with Mr. Stanco, I'll talk to him about having you join us on the trip back to Chicago."

"Fine. Yeah," Ronnie agreed. "But I'll call my dad right now." She pulled out her cell phone and dialed.

Then she waited, while Louis somehow continued to talk...about what they'd do back in Chicago, about how *his* folks had spent Christmas, about next year, next decade, next planet. Who knew. Ronnie had gone numb. She was aware of the sun shining powerlessly down, the chill all around her face and body, the tingling cold in her toes, the ice, the snow, the dull, silent door behind which Mark and his father and Mr. Stanco were brewing up a plan to kill Mayville, and the driveway and Tukamuk Lane that led out to Main, down which her father would be driving to take her away from this Stygian no-man's land.

Everything felt so...over.

17

"POP, CAN WE TALK FOR A MINUTE? Privately?"

As he waited for his father to respond, Mark saw Edward Stanco suppress a smirk and give a little nod. It was all Mark could do not to swallow the sour taste in his mouth, step towards the seated man, and drive a fist into his smug face. Except that for the last ten minutes or so of Stanco's horrible little power play, Mark had become more and more aware that it was no longer just the three of them in the room.

It was like a ghostly, amorphous crowd of people representing Mayville had silently drifted in around them as they'd talked. Like they wanted a say in how their town was going to be treated.

Mark had managed to mostly ignore their voices. Heaven knew he'd dealt with them enough in his life, both because he'd grown up here and because he'd worked for Gold Construction for most of his teens and into his twenties every summer, then full time between his undergrad and his going away to Harvard. He knew the voices. He respected them. But they were just a part of the business.

It was the last phantom person who slid into the room that finally took hold of his heart and brain and who, along with his father, was probably most responsible for his sudden shift in direction that had him challenging Stanco to his face.

Ronnie.

She'd basically made love to him then run back to her boyfriend. She'd told him point blank more than once that they could never be together. Yet he could feel her in the room with him, right there beside his heart. It was almost like he could see this discussion through her eyes, feel the rightness or wrongness of it through her heart, her skin, her volatile, demanding, *appreciation* of how things fit together.

She questioned her own judgment of things, he knew. Questioned herself, her worth, her direction in life. But Mark didn't. Somehow he could see the burning, creative core of her that was so instinctively generous he couldn't help but listen to what it said.

And it was telling him—

"Okay, Marcario," his father said, pressing himself up from his seat. "We will go into the other room." His father turned to face Stanco. "It will only be a few minutes."

"A few minutes I can wait," Stanco said and looked off, feigning boredom.

Mark's father led Mark out of the room and down the narrow hall into a second, smaller office with no windows, whose walls were covered with pinned up architectural drawings and site plans. He turned to Mark. "So?"

Mark took a deep breath. "First, I'm sorry, Pop. I—"

His father waved it off. "Big money is always a temptation."

"It wasn't the money! It was… You know what? It doesn't matter. It was a mistake to have listened to Stanco. It was a mistake not to have come to you directly with what he wanted me to do."

"Because…"

"Because you would have told me he was just looking for any way to get in to see you, get some sort of leverage on you."

Mark's father smiled sadly and reached out to put his hand on the side of Mark's face. "All true. But you heard the other things he said, didn't you? He was coming after Gold Construction with or without you."

"I just made it easier."

His father shrugged.

"We need to turn him down," Mark said.

"And ruin the company?"

"Gold won't go down. We might lose a contract or two. Might have to get smaller, like I said. But we can fight for other contracts. Despite what Stanco threatened, not everyone *likes* his approach, and not everyone will believe him if he starts spreading lies."

"The banks?"

"Stanco underestimates the power of having honest, personal dealings with them for thirty years." He held up his hands. "And no, I'm not being naïve here like I was with Stanco. We'll still have to show a plan for how GC's going to remain viable. But you know my last term requires a heavy-duty thesis, backed up by real-world studies. I plan, with your permission, to do an intensive round of bidding on contracts for GC. And if Stanco tries to pressure us out, I'm going to do everything I can to expose their dishonesty and anti-competitive practices. Make it part of my paper."

His father regarded him a long time in silence and Mark couldn't read his face. Finally his father said, "Edward Stanco is very smart, very experienced in business. Even someone as smart as you, my son, might get knocked aside. He might make it very hard for Gold, and for just you."

"But when something's right," Mark said, "you do it even if it's hard. I think you taught me that."

"Yes," Andreas Stephanopolus said, his face finally cracking a tiny smile. "As long as you do it smart, too." He reached into his pocket and pulled out his smart phone. "I have been recording everything Edward Stanco has told us so far. Let me send you the audio files."

Then, with a technological proficiency that made Mark's jaw drop in astonishment, that's exactly what Mark's father did.

~~~~

"He's a traitor and a liar," Ronnie said, staring straight ahead through the windshield of her father's Toyota pickup as he drove them home.

"You're talking about…Mark?"

Her father hadn't said anything when he'd come to get her. Just leaned over to open the passenger door for her to climb in, waited for her to close the door after her and put on her seatbelt, then spun the truck around, skidding a little on the ice of the Gold Construction parking lot, and headed out of there like he was worried someone might have seen him consorting with the devil.

Ronnie nodded, feeling the heat building up in her chest again, her palms itching like she wanted to slap something. "I'm talking about Mark. Marcario Stephanopolus. I have never been so disappointed with a person in my life."

"How so?"

She sniffed in the comfortable smell of bad coffee and donuts, one of her father's not-so-secret weaknesses that he usually indulged in when he was stressed and out driving around on his own. Maybe she *should* open up a sweets shop in this town, like Mark said. Up the quality of available guilty pleasures.

"Ronnie?"

She snapped back to the fact there wouldn't *be* a small town she'd want to be part of once Mark and his new boss got his way. "He was in league with the Stancos even when we had him over at our house and he was tearing them down just to get at Louis."

"Because he wanted to impress you."

"Maybe. Because that would get him close to you and

the town council, whose approval he'll be trying to help the Stancos get when they come in and try to suburbanize Mayville with swaths of tract housing for the workers of this big smoky furniture factory that's coming here."

"I thought—"

"I hate him. I hate Louis almost as much, though at least he never pretended to like small towns. I just want to go home and get packed."

"Packed? I thought you were staying until after New Year's."

"I'm leaving with Louis and Stanco. They may both be devils but at least they're honest ones."

"Ah. Ronnie? Are you sure…?"

And he might have said more stuff but Ronnie was now so worked up she couldn't hear anything but the accusing beat of her heart and the roar of the truck tires.

She clenched her mouth hard to keep from falling apart and pressed her head into the glass of the passenger-side window, willing her father to *Just drive, Dad. Take me home.*

~~~~

When Mark and his father and Edward Stanco spilled out into the crisp air of the GC parking lot, there was only Louis Beauchamps standing there, looking like a tall, black-wool-wrapped popsicle. Mark's elation, his burning desire to share what he'd just done with Ronnie, slipped out of him like water and all the twisting in his gut he thought he'd finally worked through with this meeting came rushing back with a vengeance.

Stanco stomped awkwardly over to Louis and swung the black lawyer's briefcase he carried like he was trying a hammer throw. Louis caught it and took it from him.

"Aren't we going to—?" Louis began.

"Let's get in the damn car and drive!" Stanco snapped.

Mark saw the understanding dawn on Louis's face. Followed by surprise, then a grudging respect and possibly pity as he looked over at Mark and his father.

"Certainly, sir," he said. "Just one thing, though…" He was obviously speaking loud enough for Mark and his father to hear and staring straight at Mark now.

"Spit it out," Stanco said.

"I'd like to drive by the Cleary house on the way out of town. Colin Cleary's daughter—you might remember her from when Colin accosted us earlier; she was the redhead with him—asked if we could give her a ride back to Chicago."

"*What?*" Mark blurted.

That put an instant visible uptick in Stanco's posture. "Colin Cleary's daughter. That's the one you're hoping to marry, isn't it? But you were facing a little competition?"

"After today," Louis said, holding Mark's gaze so hard Mark felt his heart about to pop, "I think the competition's basically done. I think she can handle the realities of business, but she has a hard time with men who lie to her and to their own fathers."

"Sounds like an interesting girl," Stanco said. "I look forward to talking with her on the ride back."

With that, he walked with Louis to the Range Rover, waited while Louis unlocked the doors, then climbed in. As the Range Rover backed up then turned and exited the parking lot, Mark's father turned to him.

"You drive after them quickly, Marcario. Go. Tell her what you have done here. Make her understand."

It was all Mark could do to stand straight, given how knotted up his insides were. "You know, Pop, if there had ever truly been a chance for the two of us, I think she would have waited to find that out for herself. Thanks for the thought, though."

"I'm telling you, Marcario, that when you get the *colpo de fulmine,* when you find the one, you don't give up. You do whatever you got to do."

"She's not the one, Pop, and I'm not in love. Now can we go back into the office and figure out the next steps for the company?"

"You are sure?"

"Absolutely."

His father shrugged and turned back to the office. Mark, fighting hard to walk without collapsing so that he only showed a slight hitch in his step, followed.

18

INTO THE NEW YEAR. A new month. Two.

On a February blah afternoon, when the sky outside Ronnie's Chicago apartment window on 70th Street East was as gray and dark and heavy as her heart, the snow a gritty gray along the sidewalks, Ronnie twirled her pen between her fingers then whacked it repeatedly against the macroeconomics text she was studying.

Her apartment smelled like apples and cinnamon from the cookies she'd baked for herself after Rolf and Chester had sent her home early. The cinnamon was supposed to rouse her spirits and help her concentrate, but all it really did was make her question, yet again, just how stupid she really was. Almost immediately after she'd returned from Mayville, she'd gone in to see Rolf and Chester and gotten their backing to re-register in U of C on a part-time basis at night to complete her BA. Masochistically, she'd chosen two economics and business electives, which were surprisingly all she needed to finish her degree.

It also turned out that they were fiendishly difficult. For

her. Her brain just did not work that way. At least when she'd studied the mathematical code of web design, there was art at the end of it. Here there were only dollars and cents. Worse, she realized the only reason she'd chosen these particular courses versus more English or web design courses had to do with trying to understand a certain someone back in Mayville whom she'd been trying to forget.

Killing herself with early workdays at Chester's and late nights attending classes and studying hadn't put that someone out of her mind either. They'd just made her tired and cranky enough that Chester had come into the back where she and Rolf were working this morning and pulled her aside.

"Why, exactly do you need a degree anyway, Smunchkin? You've done wonderful things with *our* website. And you make the best candies and marzipan this side of New York City."

"This side of anywhere," Rolf added.

"Am I good enough to set up my own shop then?" she'd snapped.

Both men had blanched. Then Rolf had pulled Chester's face into his own fleshy chest. "Our baby girl is getting ready to leave the nest!"

"Not…yet," Ronnie had said, forcing a smile. "I need to prove something first."

Chester pulled himself out of Rolf's embrace. "To whom, dearest?"

"To my parents, I guess. To show them I can do the academic thing. I *choose* to make candies."

Chester and Rolf looked at each other and Chester said, "We don't think so. Your parents are very proud of the fact you're working."

"Prove myself to Louis then. He's never liked the fact I dropped out just before finishing."

Her two bosses shook their heads.

"Myself."

"Or...?" Rolf prompted.

"Mark," she blurted. "He's in my head, calling me a coward!"

Chester nodded. He'd been the one to pull the whole story out of her on her second day back. "You need to call him."

"I can't. I still don't agree with what he did. We still don't fit. I just can't get him out of my head!"

"You mean your heart," Rolf said and gave Chester a significant look. "She means her heart."

"What*ever!*" Ronnie cried.

At which point they'd given her the afternoon off, apparently deciding she hadn't filled herself sufficiently up to the brim with love on her trip home for Christmas or something. Chester's last admonition to her as she'd left had been, "Call him."

So now Ronnie slammed closed her macroeconomics books, deciding that Keynesian theory made no sense anyway, and picked up her cell phone that she'd been obsessive about keeping charged and on her person at all times. Just in case a certain someone from Mayville should call her.

Which he had. Four times. The first three times she'd answered, chatted coldly with him. Told him she was still with Louis. And each time she waited for him to say something, she just didn't know what, exactly, that could make everything okay. She already knew that Gold Construction had turned down the deal with Stanco Bros. on the first go round. Mark explained that he'd tried to broker a deal that would have actually worked for Mayville, but that he'd had to keep the information close to his chest until the negotiations.

He said nothing about being Edward Stanco's mole inside Gold for Gold's financials. He'd said nothing about returning to Mayville only because of the Stanco deal. He said nothing about the ironclad employment agreement he'd had with the Stancos that Edward Stanco sadly explained to her on the trip back to Chicago. Or that Edward and Mark were secretly working a way around the initial refusal of Mark's father so that the Stanco-Gold partnership would proceed after all.

Mark had gone silent when she'd finally put all that to him. Then he'd calmly asked her to listen to her heart, not to half-truths and lies. Asked for her to trust him. The truth would come out.

Trust him! She so wanted to. But Louis kept sharing with her contracts that were being drawn up, minutiae of how the Stanco-Gold deal was progressing behind the scenes.

She pressed the phone book function to bring up a list of names to call and saw his.

Put the phone down.

Her mouth had gone so dry and funky that she figured she should eat another cinnamon cookie just to clear the taste, but she resisted

Picked up the phone again.

Dialed. Waited. A male voice answered.

"Hi, Dad," she said. "This is Ronnie…"

~~~~

Further east, in Boston, it was sleeting so hard that the ocean was invisible even from the shoreline. As far inland as Allston, the entire campus was a washout of falling gray ice.

Mark pulled the hood of his Adirondack further forward as he hurried up to the red brick front of Harvard's Spangler Hall. Inside the front door, he shook off his heavy backpack and brushed the spatters of rain and ice from it and from his clothes, pulled back his hood, slicked back his hair. It was a bit of a drenched and disheveled look with which to appear for his "informal review," he knew. But Ronnie probably would have liked it. It was honest.

He hurried up the stairs to the third floor and found, knocked, and entered the office they'd called him to—nondescript, but of course rimmed with heavy oak wainscoting and matching trim around the ceiling and narrow windows. The air smelled heavy, dusty, and sour, thought Mark. Maybe that was the gloomy February light and ancient overhead lamps. Maybe it was his own dread.

Four gray-haired men and one elegantly-coiffed, silver-haired woman within watched from their seats behind a long table as he entered. Three of the men were professors he'd studied with over the first three terms. The woman was presumably from the Dean's office. The fourth man looked grizzled and irascible enough to be an ethicist or part of the Harvard disciplinary board or something. None of them introduced themselves as he entered and set down his backpack and jacket beside a solid chair of dark polished wood that had been placed dead-center on the large, worn-looking Persian carpet before the table. The window lit the judgment crew from behind like they were the judgment seat of Heaven.

So be it. *Ronnie, give me strength.*

He took a deep breath, smoothed down his sweater and khaki pants, and sat.

The first one to speak was Professor Krizansky, a brilliant, almost-uncomfortably-handsome little man with a straight, sculpted nose and every silver hair always carefully in place. He had taught Mark in Innovations in Business, Energy, and Environment last term. Mark suspected it was him who'd suggested Mark for an academic award, based on Mark's paper on sustainable building methods. And it was probably him who was most upset by what Mark assumed was Edward Stanco making good on his personal threats.

Krizansky shuffled his papers in front of him on the table and began very formally. "Mr. Stephanopolus, I'm guessing from your expression that you have some idea why you've been summoned here."

"Does it have to do with communications from Edward Stanco?" Mark said.

"Yes."

"Charges of plagiarism?"

Krizansky shared a significant look with the other faculty and administration members seated behind the table. Then he turned his gaze back to Mark. Krizansky was a vigorous man in his fifties, widely read, empathetic, and more keyed into global and environmental issues than any other business professor Mark had encountered at Harvard. Mark felt like they'd had an instant connection during their classroom debates.

Krizansky didn't look particularly sympathetic now. His fine brows were down and his pale blue eyes flashed dangerously as he asked, "And how, Mr. Stephanopolus, do you know that Edward Stanco has charged you with plagiarism?"

"Am I going to be given the opportunity to directly confront my accuser?"

Krizansky shook his head. "This is not a court of law, Mr. Stephanopolus. It's not even an official hearing at this point. It's just an informal meeting to discuss what happened and what our school standards are. And I repeat: how do you know that Edward Stanco charged you with plagiarism?"

Here it was, Ronnie. Time to see whether full and honest disclosure actually *was* the best way to live one's life in this world.

"It's an educated guess," Mark said, "because he threatened he would do as much, write his own version of my paper and backdate it, whatever it took to make it look legitimate, to punish me if I did not carry out what he considered our 'deal' over the Christmas holidays."

Krizansky's eyebrows went up. "Your 'deal?'"

So Mark laid it out for them.

~~~~

"Hey, darling."

Her father's warm greeting almost made Ronnie buckle. She had, of course, spoken with her parents numerous times since her hurried departure after Christmas. She'd never mentioned Mark or his business, though, and her parents had delicately never brought it up.

Even now, she started her conversation with her dad casually, telling him she was just in a bit of a funk, what with all the work and school and gloomy February weather.

By the time her father got through all the family news, though, explaining that her mother would come to the phone except that she was out at a book club she'd joined, Ronnie was ready to burst.

"And, um, the Putter's Ridge project we saw?" she said lightly. "Have the Stanco Brothers shown up on site yet?"

There was a delay on the other end of the line and Ronnie

wondered whether her cell had lost a connection.

"Dad?"

"I'm here, dear. Just wondering how much you actually want to know about all of this."

She forced a laugh. "Well let's start with how Mayville's town council is handling it." He'd been elected almost by acclamation a couple weeks ago and Ronnie had called to congratulate him then.

"We're not. Yet."

"Really? Why? The Woodwand thing got delayed or something?"

"Or something."

"Dad! Come on."

"You want to know about Mark, I guess."

"I didn't... Yeah. I guess."

There was another pause, then her father cleared his throat. "Gold Construction decided not to partner with Stanco Brothers after all. Mark's doing, apparently. According to Andreas, Mark has risked his entire career and Andreas might have risked his company. Stanco pretty much promised to squash them both."

"You believe that? You don't think Mark may be continuing to deal privately with the Stancos?"

She could almost hear her father's consternation on the phone. "Not sure when you lost your ability to judge character, hon, or if it's just your feelings for Mark have thrown you off, but I believe what Andreas told me."

An electric charge rushed through Ronnie, taking her breath with it. She licked her dry lips, swallowed, and forced herself to breathe again. She wasn't sure if she was elated or terrified. Maybe a bit of both. "What exactly did Andreas say?"

"He...said he'd been ready to follow his son down whatever road Mark wanted to take them. He trusts his son with the future of the company." Ronnie's father had to stop for a moment to collect himself. "And he said he was very proud that Mark stood up to Edward Stanco, whatever the consequences."

"Which are what?" Ronnie pressed. "Isn't Mark back at Harvard for his final term?"

"I believe so. Though Andreas said Mark's also been doing a lot of hustling around, too. He's been visiting all of Gold's suppliers and contracts and their banker, doing what he can to make sure they stick with them. It might be a bit of a David and Goliath fight he's gotten his father into, but...you know...I'm almost tempted this time to bet on the little guy."

Ronnie laughed though it stuck in her throat. "You always do, Dad. You taught me that. But you also taught me that they don't always win. You have to face reality too."

"You do, my darling. You do." He paused. "So how are you and Louis doing?"

~~~~

By the time Mark had explained his "deal" with Edward Stanco, gone through the genesis of his paper, pulled out and presented his research on the usual building methods Stanco Brothers used, and, finally showed them the two versions of the possible Putter's Ridge partnership—the one he'd proposed versus the one Edward Stanco had come back to them with—Mark was sure any fair-minded person would have a pretty clear idea of just what had transpired here.

He was disappointed, then, to see a clearly sympathetic posture in only Krizansky and one of the other professors before him. Or maybe he shouldn't have been surprised. He knew from experience how persuasive Edward Stanco could be. And he didn't doubt that Stanco Brothers had probably sponsored more than a few Harvard Business School events over the years.

Professor Krizansky could obviously read the mood of the others as well as Mark could and turned a sympathetic eye on Mark.

"You can understand, Mr. Stephanopolus, how your whole story of a secret deal with Mr. Stanco might be suspect. Since it accuses him of unethical behavior, it might even be considered slander."

Mark swallowed. "I don't believe his dealing with me in secret to find common ground with my father was unethical. I do believe him falsely accusing me of plagiarism was. Is. And my saying so in an 'informal' meeting is certainly not slander, particularly when it's the simple truth."

Krizansky looked at the others, who'd started muttering among themselves, then was about to address Mark again when the grizzled man with a deeply-etched frown held up a hand.

"You know, Mr. Stephanopolus, over the years we've had any number of smart young men and women up here, defending themselves against charges of plagiarism. And most times the student simply claims complete lack of awareness of the source they're said to have copied. Your defense is at least aggressive and original. It's just not believable."

Mark's worry and embarrassment was morphing inside him now to something he vaguely recognized as more dangerous—a slow burning anger. He fixed his gaze on the grizzled man and asked. "Just what part of my story, sir, is not believable?"

The old man blinked, sputtered a moment, then sat back with a smile, looking at his peers with a casual disbelief. Finally he turned back to Mark. "You cooked up a pretty good story of how you came up with your paper. Reasonable. But when you're confronted with evidence that Edward Stanco, who you *admit* you've had some adversarial dealings with, presents proof that you copied it, lifting entire passages verbatim, from something he himself wrote almost a year ago, the best you can say is that he doesn't like you? You think the CEO of a company the size of Stanco Bros. gives a flea shit in hell's thought what a Harvard student working for his father's tiny, two bit building company out in the Midwest does or doesn't do?"

"He flew and drove out to our little 'two bit' building company in the middle of winter to negotiate a deal with us," Mark said.

The old man wrinkled his nose. "You yourself said he had another deal going in a nearby town. You were probably a side trip."

"Actually, I could bring you evidence that he flew into Chicago and drove through two hours on some pretty bad roads strictly to meet with us, and drove straight back, but even that, I suspect would just make you shrug. One more bit of circumstantial evidence. But I am going to take you at your word that your main hurdle here is my assertion that the CEO of a company as big as Stanco could possibly care enough about a small, midwest building company to do something unethical to hurt them. Or me."

He shot a glance at Krizansky. "I'm also going to take you at your word that this is not a court of law but a group that truly wants to determine the truth. To that end I'm going to present something I've considered holding back because it hasn't been run through a panel of evidence experts—though I'm certainly open to doing that if necessary—and it does contain some semi-confidential business information."

Mark looked at each of the panel judges and saw he had their full attention.

"My father, more experienced in dealing with businessmen like Edward Stanco, secretly taped the December 28th meeting I told you about. I think the last thirty minutes of it are sufficient to get a sense of what went on."

He reached down to where he'd left his backpack and pulled out his smartphone and the exterior speakers he'd brought for the occasion. He hooked them together, switched to the audio file his father had sent him, and pressed Play.

~~~~

"Louis and I?" Ronnie said to her father over the phone line. "Um…fine."

"Just 'fine?' He proposed to you when you were here a couple months ago. Thought you'd have set a date by now."

"I've been busy."

"Work and school. I know. You've been busy. Mark's been busy. How's Louis been?"

Ronnie felt her serious mood crack at last. "Busy."

Her father chuckled. "You know, hon, I wasn't particularly happy when you were here over Christmas. The way you seemed to be flipping back and forth between two guys. Obviously upset over Louis about something. No, no, don't tell me. I don't want to know."

"But you suspect."

"I'm still a lawyer. That's my job. But you worked through it, right?"

"Through what? The thing with Louis?" Ronnie chewed on her lip for a moment. *Had* she? "Well, we haven't slept together since then."

"Whoah! Whoah, my darling! Too much information. But…why?"

Ronnie shrugged. "Like I said, we've both been really really busy."

"It's not because of Mark?"

"Because of…" She let it trail off. Count on her father to state the obvious that she wouldn't even admit to herself. Of course it was because of Mark. Even more, now that she knew he'd done the right thing regarding a deal with Stanco. And triply, since she'd heard how he was struggling to deal with the aftereffects of that decision.

"You ever consider just, I don't know, calling him?" her father said.

"What?"

"That's what Alex asked me about when I talked to him yesterday. Asked whether you'd been in contact with him."

"Nosy brother."

"Oh, I just think Alex likes Mark a lot more than Louis."

"No doubt."

"Sees himself playing hockey each winter with him at family reunions. Maybe baseball in the summer…"

"Dad! Even if Louis and I don't marry, which…which I can't guarantee, I still don't see how Mark and I would ever get together. We want different things out of life."

"Really?" Her father sounded way too interested, which made all of Ronnie's warning shields go up. "What things, exactly, *do* you want out of life, dear?"

"Oh, you know, just working. Learning…"

"Opening a candy shop of your own one day."

"You actually believe I could?"

"I think—"

"Mark thought I could. He said…a lot of things."

"I think Mark's got pretty good judgment."

"Maybe."

"Would it be in Mayville?"

Ronnie sighed. "There's not enough *traffic* there, Dad. You need a certain critical population for the sort of place I'd want to do. Mayville falls short of it. Just short. But short. And it's probably going to stay that way if, as you say, Stanco and Woodwand aren't moving in."

"Looked into it, have you?"

"I— Maybe."

"Because of Mark?"

"In my stupider moments, I think… You know that, regardless of what happens or whatever else he might want to do with his life, he's pretty much tied to his father's company and to Mayville. That kind of trap isn't something I can deal with. I don't like being forced down someone else's road."

"Hm." There was a long silence on the phone and Ronnie wondered whether her father had somehow gotten distracted or drifted off or something. Then he said. "Seems to me that there's a world of difference between being forced down a certain road and being invited to join someone on their journey."

Now it was Ronnie's turn to be silent.

"The town's just not big enough," she said at last.

"Mm-hm."

"There's no good place there for the kind of upscale sweets shop I'd want to do."

"Probably true."

"Even if I did *everything* right, do you have any idea of the failure rate for that kind of enterprise?"

"That something you're studying in your business courses?"

"Among other things."

"Well then maybe you're right. Maybe there's no way for you to ever open a successful business like that in Mayville. Like you said, Mayville's prospects aren't looking so hot anymore, and Mark's going to be staying here regardless…"

"What Mark Stephanopolus does or doesn't do isn't important!" Ronnie said.

"Right. Right. Of course not. Though he's still trying to see if Woodwand will come to Mayville with just Gold Construction handling the housing needs here."

"What? He's…he's…how?"

"Direct meetings, apparently. Same thing he's been doing with a number of former Gold Construction clients who've been somehow convinced to pull contracts from GC. I think I heard through the grapevine, in fact, that Louis Beauchamps was involved in some of those reversals. He's apparently deeply involved in trying to woo Woodwand to another plant location, in fact."

"So?" Ronnie said, almost sputtering. "I thought you hated development. You wouldn't have wanted Woodwand to come to Mayville anyway, would you?"

"Actually, Woodwand submitted a proposal before Edward Stanco and Louis threw their hooks deep into them. I was pretty impressed. They're basically everything Mark said they are."

"And Louis... Mark never told me about any of this."

"You mean after you drove off on him without saying goodbye?"

"He's...called a few times. I told him I was still with Louis."

"I guess he sensed you didn't want to be forced down the road he's chosen."

"I guess not." She paused and swallowed a very bad taste that she could only assume was her body's way of turning to liquid every bad feeling of stupidity and guilt she felt and shoving it into her mouth through her salivary glands. "Dad, you know you can be pretty harsh."

"I know I can, darling," he said softly. "But sometimes you kids really need a good slap upside your heads."

"Gee, thanks."

"You're welcome."

"Give my love to Mom. I have to make another phone call now."

She hung up, and speed-dialed Louis Beauchamp.

~~~~

Back on the east coast, in the third floor room of Spangler Hall, Harvard Business School, Mark was on his feet behind the chair where he was supposed to be sitting. But it was really the smartphone and speakers Mark had placed there which were the center of attention now. And Mark had been too steamed to sit still when he heard Stanco say again, "That's going to cost you, kid," then casually detail all the illegal, anticompetitive acts the Stanco Bros. could do to destroy the company Mark's father had built.

Now Mark's fingers clutched the back of the wooden chair as the audio playback wrapped up. "One way or another, Andreas," Edward Stanco's voice grated out through the speakers, "the Stancos always get what we want."

Mark bent down, thumbed off the audio file player, then looked up at the table of judges to see the grizzled man's face had actually gone pale. Mark cleared his throat. "After this, I consulted with my father in private. Then we came out to tell Mr. Stanco we were not going to deal with him after all."

"You say 'we' came out to tell Mr. Stanco," Krizansky said. "Who delivered that decision to him? Was it you or your father?"

"Does that matter?"

"Just curious."

"Given my former dealings with Mr. Stanco, my father let me speak on his behalf."

"Because speaking out for what you believe is right is important to you, isn't it, Mr. Stephanopolus? Enough to do it here. Maybe enough to do it outside of this small room?"

"Myron!" cried the woman behind the judge's table.

"What Stanco actually did— It's not an actionable offence!" offered Professor Torres, who Mark remembered covering a section on contract law in his business development course.

"It...might be," said the grizzled man, then shot a look at Mark. "But it wouldn't be wise."

Krizansky seemed to be fighting hard to hide a smile as he took in the strained faces of his colleagues. He turned back to Mark.

"I think that concludes this hearing, Mr. Stephanopolus. We'll communicate our decision to you by Friday at the latest."

19

THE BEGINNING OF MARCH in Chicago was every bit as cold as February had been, so that Ronnie was surprised, looking at things with a business eye as she wiped gummy syrup off her taffy-making stovetop to head off for class, at how non-seasonal the business at Chester's Sweets was.

Located along Chicago's "Magnificent Mile", Chester's was flooded in the summer, of course. Also during celebrations like Christmas, Valentine's Day, and Mother's. But there seemed to be a devoted crowd of addicts who worked in the downtown core who kept the shop humming through the darkest, snowiest, dreariest days.

Or maybe the need to fight that gloom was precisely why those addicts kept coming. She got that. She could still hear the customers out front, those with earlier quitting hours, oohing and ahing over the display cases while Chester bustled around and Mandy, their part-timer answered questions and handled sales. This place was celebration, filled today with Rolf's chocolate-and-cream scents of relaxation, and the vanilla-nutmeg scent of the taffy she'd just made.

It was come-in-from-the-blah-weather magic. An oasis of light and warmth and good smells. A place to love life.

Which made it all the more painful when she had to leave it each day.

Thumping her rags and full-front apron in the laundry bin, she double-checked that her various burners were off and hurried to the other side of the kitchen to give Rolf a kiss before grabbing her coat and boots, tugging on a warm hat and gloves, and hurrying out through the front of the shop to head for the Hyde Park Express bus going down State Street. She waved to Chester and Mandy. If Ronnie was lucky, she'd catch one right away and be at the campus in just over half an hour.

She made it out the front door and two steps south along the sidewalk before someone grabbed her by her arm and she shrieked, whirling instinctively to slug her assailant.

"Whoah! Ron-Ron!" Louis cried, catching her punch and turning it to whirl her in close. Like a dance move. Like she was part of it, not filled with a steam-puffing, heart-racing panic at his sudden appearance here.

"What—what are you *doing* here?"

"A guy can't pick up his fiancée from work?"

"I'm not— I thought I told you, I'm never going to marry someone whose sole job is trying to ruin someone's business. And take your hands off me."

He released her. "You mean Gold Construction."

"I mean Gold Construction and Mark Stephanopolus. Yes."

He stepped closer to the painted wood and brick that fronted Chester's and pulled her back with him to allow a bunch of very-intense, after-work business men and women to push their way by on the sidewalk. "You don't know, then," he said.

"Know what?"

"What your childhood swim buddy has done."

Ronnie frowned at him. "What do you mean?"

Louis held up his gloved hands in open supplication. His face looked gray in the gloomy light. "You're right. Representing Edward Stanco, I convinced Woodwand to pull back on its plans to set up down in Mayville. *And* I've been helping to win away a bunch of contracts that might have otherwise gone to Gold Construction."

"But how did you win them away, Louis? Hunh?"

He shrugged. "Better deals. Cheaper labor."

"Loss leaders? Charging below cost? Isn't that called monopolistic behavior or something?"

"Or something, maybe. The fact is Stanco Brothers offers contracts with fewer environmental and quality costs. Closer to national building standards, actually."

"And you *never* talked down Gold Construction or the Stephanopoluses, right?"

"The point is, Ronnie, that your golden boy struck back."

Ronnie looked up and down the bustle of Michigan Avenue, looking for a quick escape route. "I've heard. He's holding face-to-face meetings. Trying to convince the contracts to come back."

"Is that what he told you? Oh no, he's gone much nastier."

She frowned at Louis. "How?"

"Social media. Who'd have thunk, hunh? Must be something they're teaching in school now."

"Social media?" So *not.* At least not the business school professors Ronnie had met. But how was Mark using—

"He apparently recorded some of the negotiations he and his dad had with Edward Stanco back in January, conducted in private, with the reasonable expectation of same, and posted clips of them on a web page, linked to a new Facebook page, Twitter account, LinkedIn, Tumbler, HotBuzz, whatever. All that along with some pretty outrageous claims about the Stanco Brothers."

Wow. "Outrageous as in false?"

Louis looked at her with an expression of honest shock. She just didn't know if it was shock over the idea that one of his clients might actually warrant all the things being said about him, or shock that Ronnie was actually standing up to him. Again. It felt good.

"Whether they're true or not, Ronnie," Louis said slowly and carefully, as if she were a child, "what he's done is career suicide. You don't go publicly slandering someone as big as Edward Stanco and think he won't come back at you. Stanco is lining up a passel of litigation lawyers from my firm as we speak. I'm afraid Mark won't know what hit him."

Ronnie fought off a sudden wave of fear that gripped her around her chest, but she stared down at the sidewalk and mumbled, "It's not slander if it's true."

"Oh, Ronnie. I hope you don't seriously believe that will save Mark? Quite aside from the costs of litigation, which will bankrupt both Gold Construction and Mark personally, by the time this trial is done, Mark will have been painted in the national newspapers as such a calculating, bitter, weasel that no businessman in his right mind would ever want to be caught dead doing a deal with him. Even if he wins. It'll be what the phrase *Pyrrhic victory* was made for."

She raised her chin back up, forcing herself to breathe. "Is that what you came here to tell me? Because I have a class to get to, you know."

"That's... No, what I came here to *ask* of you, is that you come out to dinner with me tonight."

He obviously saw her shock that he could be so crass. He held up his hands. "Before you say no, just hear me out. Edward Stanco is back in town and he and I have a dinner meeting tonight with Carl Hemsler, the CEO and Chairman of Woodwand Furniture. Hemsler has apparently seen Mark's internet campaign and has some questions about Stanco Brothers now."

Someone bumped Ronnie as they passed and she barely noticed. She was intensely studying Louis, trying to figure out what the game was. "What does that have to do with me?"

Louis smiled. "Don't you see? Edward Stanco likes you.

From our drive back to Chicago together in December. He knows you're not crazy about his business practices, that you felt like he'd attacked your hometown. He gets that. And he knows you've got a thing for Mark Stephanopolus too. We both get that."

Ronnie found herself blushing hotly, but wasn't sure if she was angry or embarrassed by Louis baldly stating what she had trouble admitting even to herself.

"The thing is, Ronnie, Edward needs a simple chance to prove to the larger business community that he'd not the rapacious, amoral slickster that Mark has made him out to be. And he figures that if he can get one high-profile, known-to-be-highly-ethical company like Woodwand to hire Stanco Brothers as their close building partner, he can turn the tide of public opinion."

"And you honestly thought I'd want to help you with—"

"Oh, of course not. I imagine you probably hate Stanco Brothers right now. Maybe you even think you hate me, though I'm hopeful that will pass. But I do know you better than you even know yourself, Ronnie. I know, for instance, that you probably feel guilty for walking out on Mark when he was about to do the quote-unquote 'right thing.' And you think you love him. And you know, like I do, that they guy's got a stubborn moral streak that's not going to let him settle things with the Stancos. Which means he's going to go to court and destroy both his life and his family's."

"Unless he wins the Woodwand contract back. That will

save Gold Construction and—"

"No. Sorry, Ron. It won't. The halo effect of Gold might help the Stancos if they get it, but it's not enough for a company being dragged under by litigation. Gold won't have the time or resources to fulfill anything they sign with Woodwand. Which means Woodwand ultimately withdraws and both Gold and Mark Stephanopolus go under."

He let it lie there, not trying to defend the ruthlessness of it, or its inevitability. Just letting Ronnie soak it in, really understand what Mark had called down on himself. And Ronnie did, feeling the weight of it so heavy she could hardly breathe.

"Unless," she said at last, "I go out with you tonight and betray Mark by convincing Woodwand to go with Stanco Brothers."

Louis nodded. "If it works, and the tide of public opinion turns…"

"No." Ronnie swallowed and looked up at the blue sky above her as she'd found herself doing a lot lately, wondering if Mark felt the connection it gave them. "If I agree to do this, I want a contract in writing that says Edward Stanco won't go after Mark and Gold Construction in court."

"If you agree to do this and you *convince* Carl Hemsler to get Woodwand working with Stanco Brothers…"

"Fine! In writing."

Louis smiled and leaned forward to peck her cheek. "I'll see what I can do."

~~~~

In the Tea Shoppe in Harvard Square near Brattle and Massachusetts Avenue, Mark was hunched over a steaming cup of Ceylon Vanilla tea, his back to most of the cozy collection of tall black tables and bar-stool chairs, his eyes scanning the outside gray—gray skies, gray paving stones, gray couples linked arm in arm as they walked from glittering shop to shop.

In front of him, on the elevated faux-wood counter that ran along the front window, he'd spread out his course materials on leadership, trying to find some practical guidance for handling the attention his private war with Stanco Brothers was suddenly getting in the traditional media. It was both threatening the Sustainable Business Ideas group he'd started at the business school and charging it up at the same time.

He'd never really planned to be a leader in the school. He'd just tried to study, learn, and simultaneously fight for the health of his father's business. But doing the last of these had required expanding himself in all sorts of ways. He'd had to reach out for help to the more technologically gifted of his classmates to get the social media stuff going (though he'd *wanted* to call Ronnie, and had almost broached the subject the last time he'd spoken with her). He'd corralled a former lawyer who'd come to Harvard for his MBA to keep him on the right side of legal. He'd even formed alliances with a bunch of the environmental activists in the school to suss out just what the earth issues were with the Stanco Brothers' usual business practices.

Somehow all the people he'd worked with had coalesced into a group for whom the Stanco Bros. affair was only the catalyst. He'd casually suggested they name themselves the SBI group and it had leapt into being, just like that, with him at the head.

The Stanco Bros. battle was far from done, but now it was only one of a number of companies they were bringing into the light.

At least, he thought as he sat back from the spread-out papers before him and cradled his steaming ceramic mug of vanilla tea, he had enough brilliant people in SBI that it wasn't a problem implementing any plans they came up with. He was just supposed to kind of *guide* all that brilliance. Be their moral compass, as it were.

Which was weird, because he felt like his personal moral compass was living almost exactly one thousand miles away, in Chicago, Illinois. And she wasn't talking to him.

"I'm crazy," he murmured into his mug of tea.

"Talking to yourself like that? You just might be."

Mark jerked upright so quickly his tea sloshed over the side of his mug, burned his hand, and he barely managed to keep himself from yelling out and dropping the mug onto the floor.

"Sorry," said Professor Krizansky, who'd appeared at

his shoulder to hear his self-analysis. "Never startle a man holding hot tea."

"Professor." Mark set his mug carefully onto the counter between his spread out papers and turned, wiping his hand on the cotton sweater he wore.

"Call me Myron, please. I think you've earned that right, outside of school and given you're not even taking a class with me this term."

"Sure thing, Professor."

Krizansky shrugged and looked over his spread-out papers and leadership textbook. "Leadership? Seems to me you could be *teaching* this stuff about now. What are you looking for?"

"Ways to handle mainstream media blowback."

"Have you talked to Andrea Lebreque? First year. Background in NBC public relations."

Mark scribbled down the name. "Thank you."

Krizansky nodded. "But the circles under your eyes aren't about that, I'm thinking."

"Excuse me?"

Krizansky pulled up the nearest bar stool seat and sat at the counter beside Mark, looking out, as Mark had done, across the meandering bustle in the square outside. The light had gone down enough, Mark saw, that all the stores and restaurants had turned on their exterior lights and the scene looked actually warmer than it had before. A reminder of Christmas somehow.

"I've been watching you, Mark," Krizansky said. "I've watched you turn from having a massive chip on your shoulder when you first arrived at Harvard to being someone that other students, and even staff, turn to for inspiration because you just seem to have it all figured out. Your life, I mean. Your values. You give to others. You also ask things of them that make them step up to their own better selves. It's rarer than you think."

Mark felt a slow heat creeping up his neck, a very unfamiliar sensation.

"But what I don't think others see," Krizansky continued, "is how time-specific the change has been, and how, when you're not calling others up or racing around being a paragon, you look kind of…bereft."

Mark blinked, feeling suddenly very exposed, the tingling heat in his neck now moved all the way up the back of his head and took over his scalp.

"Now it's possible," Krizansky said, turning his pale blue gaze directly on Mark, "that you just had some spiritual revelation. It all happened over the Christmas break, after all. Or it was all caused by the dust-up you had with Edward Stanco over that break? But I'm guessing that was only part of it. In fact, given the way I've seen you moon around when you think no one's noticing, I'd guess there's a girl involved. Pardon me, I mean, *woman*."

Mark felt another little jolt. Noting Krizansky's handsome face again, his perfect nose, perfect hair, pale blue eyes, Mark suddenly wondered if—

Krizansky chuckled. "I've been married twenty-eight years, Mark. Still madly in love. And I recognize the signs, that's all. Who is she?"

"A…childhood friend," Mark found himself blurting. Then he suddenly spilled the entire tale, not sure why he could confess it all to this former professor of his, but still feeling immensely relieved that he could.

When he'd finished, Krizansky paid him the respect of not making some glib comment, but actually sat and thought through the story Mark had just told him.

~~~~

The dinner Louis took Ronnie to was in a new, very chichi restaurant call Chandeliers. It had a snooty Eurotrash ambiance, with polished cement floors, steel tables, and a middle-of-the-room gas fireplace held by an all-white column of sculpted Corian material.

Ronnie felt, as she stood in the vestibule while Louis spoke to the maître d', that she was entering the gullet of some kind of sci-fi space whale.

Her comfort level was already redlining in the white, insanely-tight, ankle-length Dior dress and stiletto heels Louis had also bought for her, whisking her straight from their meeting out front of Chester's to a private couturier who'd obviously been briefed that she'd be coming.

"I feel like a B-movie harlot," she whispered to Louis now as he returned to her and gave her his arm to lead her in.

"You do look like a movie star," Louis whispered back. "Edward has it on good authority that it's a particular weakness of Carl Hemsler. The man's happily married, devout, and thoroughly Midwest, but secretly devours celebrity rags and TV shows. We figure your stunning looks, this dress, and your natural cornpone charm, will make you his wet dream come to life."

"Is that supposed to be flattering?"

He checked his step for a half beat, and looked at her seriously. "Ronnie, I'm sorry. I just mean that you're absolutely beautiful tonight. You're *my* wet dream and my soul dream. You always have been. I think there's just a part of me that wants to let the whole world know that."

Ronnie nodded, knowing that what Louis said was at least partly true. He'd judged her attractive and figured he could get some mileage out of that. "I'm here because of the contract you got Edward to sign. That's all, Louis. Keep it in your pants."

She smiled sadly as they resumed their walk and reached the table where two men quickly stood to greet them.

Edward Stanco was his usual skeletal, pointy-faced self in another expensive dark suit. The new man, introduced by Stanco as Carl Hemsler, CEO and Chairman of Woodwand Furniture, was a balding, dough-faced man with sweaty palms, who nonetheless radiated a surprising aura of friendly goodness.

After a round of introductions, they all ordered meals. Despite the cold ambiance of the room, the food was surprisingly good, served sizzling fresh for the prawn-and-scallop stir-fry Louis ordered, suitably bloody for the steaks the other two men ordered, and with an authentic peanut crunch for the Thai-inspired grilled chicken dish Ronnie ordered for herself.

That and the good merlot—if there was one thing she did love about eating out with Louis was his taste in wine—made sitting down with two men who'd been actively trying to ruin Gold Construction and a third who'd, on their word, backed away from investing in Mayville completely, almost bearable.

Until all the Midwestern talk about the weather and how the men had found their way there was all used up, and even asking Ronnie about her unusual profession was done. Then, as the main meal was done and they were waiting for some coffee and chilled chocolate mousse, Stanco finally brought them all back to the purpose of the dinner.

Ronnie listened to his pitch and marveled at how such a morally and physically repulsive man could come across as so charming and reasonable. Throw in a real need to believe what he was selling and Ronnie finally began to understand how Mark had been talked into scouting out the opportunities for a Stanco Bros.-Gold Construction alliance.

"Ultimately," Stanco was saying as Louis's thumb to her thigh brought Ronnie's attention fully back to the table, "bringing Woodwand to Lonsdon will give you all the benefits you would have found in Mayville, but you'll be working with us. We can build you whatever you need in half the time, and there's no problem with scaling it up or down as we go."

Hemsler now looked embarrassed. He brought his napkin up from his lap to wipe his mouth. "Um…yeah. The only issue I see? Well, like you let me know about Gold when we were going to go to Mayville, I've been reading a bunch of stuff about you and yours online, Ed. Things about clearcutting? And basically dumping ecological regulations?"

Stanco gave an easy smile. "Have to consider the source for those, though, don't you. Where'd you read those things?"

Hemsler frowned. "I'm…I'm not exactly sure. Seems to me it was in the paper I read. Also got sent some articles by some business friends of mine. And of course that recording of your meeting with Andreas Stephanopolus and his son."

He threw the last one out like a direct challenge, his lower lip thrusting, quivering a bit.

"Ah, yes. The so-called 'recording.' Pretty amazing what a good sound engineer can create out of various sound samples, isn't it."

"You're saying it was faked?" Hemsler looked dubious.

"I'm not saying that I didn't meet with Stephanopolus and son. Of course I did. To work out a way we could, *together*, help Woodwand come to Mayville. Some of that 'recording' the son secretly made of our meeting is actually accurate. The plan they'd put forward was so pie-in-the-sky I was almost embarrassed for them. But I never threatened them or even implicitly did so. Louis can vouch for that. He sat in on that meeting. Louis?"

Ronnie, who clearly remembered being in the car with Louis, driving around town with him, then standing in the parking lot with him while he called her father to come and get her, now turned, like Hemsler to look at Louis. "Is that right, Louis?" she asked.

He didn't miss a beat. "Absolutely. I was sitting there with Mr. Stanco the whole time, taking notes, ready to draw up the final agreement. There were no threats. I was honestly shocked when Mr. Stanco played me this supposed recording that someone had found on the internet."

Louis paused, smiling smoothly at Hemsler. "What Mr. Stanco is being too much of a gentleman to say, though, is that the Stephanopolus son had extra motivations to launch all these spurious attacks on Stanco Bros."

"Really?" Carl Hemsler was all ears now. "What extra motivations?"

Louis sighed and looked at Ronnie. "Her. The Stephanopolus son apparently had, still has, a major crush on her, which I fully understand. He'd hoped to score a huge coup, brokering a deal between his father's company and Mr. Stanco. Would have made him a big man in town. Figured it might have convinced Ms. Cleary to give up her Chicago dreams and move back to Mayville to be with him. But because he lied to his father about it initially, and to her, and to everyone around him, it seems, that really wasn't going to work. Not to mention the fact she was already engaged to me."

He shot a smile to Ronnie that she could barely process through her amazement at the web of lies he wove so casually. How had she believed *anything* he'd ever told her before?

"So when the deal fell apart and he also found Ms. Cleary had left, Mark Stephanopolus went a little off the rails. He started up this smear campaign which Mr. Stanco has been struggling over how to deal with. I've recommended *litigation*, of course…"

Stanco broke in. "But I'd just as soon not ruin the kid's future. I figure if we can just keep on doing good business, like the deal we strike with Woodwand tonight, the lies will eventually just fade away."

"Lies," said Carl Hemsler. "Hunh." Then he sat back in his chair, mulling it all over, before turning to Ronnie, just as Stanco and Louis had set him up to do. "Ms. Cleary," he said. "Ronnie? I actually met your father in Mayville and I was impressed by his sense of integrity. Have to say you strike me as falling pretty close to the tree, despite you being a whole lot better looking. So you tell me to go with Mr. Stanco here, and I'll go with Mr. Stanco. Deal or no deal?"

Deal meant Stanco left Mark alone. *Deal* meant Ronnie would have done what she could to repay the wrong she'd done to Mark by simply walking out on him without saying goodbye. *Deal* meant Mark could look after his father in Mayville, while Ronnie lived her life here. Like she should.

"Carl…" She reached over and put a hand on Hemsler's

forearm. Bless him for keeping his eyes on hers and not checking out her cleavage. "How you ever believed what these two snakes told you about Gold Construction I'll never know. Louis Beauchamp and Edward Stanco are, without a doubt, two of the biggest lying, ruthless, amoral businessmen I've ever met and you would be betraying everything you and your company stand for if you did business with them."

"Ronnie!" Louis snapped.

"They got me to come out here on the threat of suing my friend and ruining his life and his father's company with that lawsuit," Ronnie said. "But I think I'd rather trust the court's ability to find the truth than be a party to their lies even one minute more."

She took off her impossible-to-walk-on stilletos, held them and the bottom of her dress in one hand, and stood up. To Louis, she said, "Don't call me again. Don't track me down at home or at work or I'll get a restraining order."

And she left.

~~~~

"It sounds to me," Krizansky said at last, tapping a finger thoughtfully beside Mark's now-empty mug of vanilla tea, "that you need to have a certain degree of patience and trust here."

Mark crossed his arms over his chest, surprised. "What? I

shouldn't *go* for it? I shouldn't find a way to work in Chicago? Or forget the girl and just move on with my life?"

"Do any of those options sound like they have a high probability of achieving your ultimate objective?"

"What's my ultimate objective?"

Krizansky tilted his head. "You're asking me?"

"Put yourself in my shoes. What would be the best possible outcome?"

Krizansky smiled. "Happiness. Fulfillment. Living your life fully with a wife who's living her life fully as well."

"And if that's not possible?"

Mark winced as his former professor clapped a hand on his shoulder and stood. "Oh, I'm sure you've thought through just how it might be possible, Mr. Stephanopolus. I suspect a part of everything you've done since you met this woman has been geared towards making it possible. You just don't know if any of your efforts are going to pay off."

Mark looked down at his empty tea mug. "Even if she doesn't marry Louis, there's no guarantee she'll come back to me. You got a business formula for that one?"

"Business is easy, Mr. Stephanopolus. But it's true love that really counts."

"Faith and trust?"

Krizansky pointed his index finger at him, then slipped away through the Tea Shoppe crowd and out.

20

THREE MORE MONTHS OF HELL. That's what the separation felt like to Ronnie. Three months of quietly watching from the sidelines as the man she could not wipe from her heart engaged in a pitched, and very public, public relations and legal battle with Edward Stanco and his company.

She'd called him after the fiasco dinner with Stanco, Louis, and Hemsler, just to give him a heads up on what she'd done, what the possible fallout might be.

Also that she was listening to her heart now, but still needed some time and space to work things out. If he could wait. If he didn't forget her in the whirlwind his life had become.

Then, during a brief quiet time during the June afternoon of Ronnie's graduation from the University of Chicago, Alex casually guided her to a recent business article he'd found on the internet:

20 May 2014

Five Harvard Business School Students Win the Dean's Award for Service to the School, Business Community, and Society

BOSTON—In a year filled with impressive students attending the country's most prestigious business school, five students of the Harvard Business School MBA class of 2014 were honored with the Dean's Award for extraordinary leadership and contributions to the school and greater community. Established in 1997, the Dean's Award is presented yearly to a varying number of students nominated from among Harvard Business School community. This year, the winners are Janice Powell, Sandra Ghandi, Mark Stephanopolus, Kirsten Chang, and Gordon Collette. They were formally recognized by the dean at Tuesday's commencement ceremonies.

JANICE POWELL comes from a background of social...

Ronnie, disturbed by the obvious beauty and accomplishments of Janice and Sandra, and annoyed that she was disturbed, found her way down to the passage about Mark.

MARK STEPHANOPOLUS is the son of an immigrant house builder who plans to take over and grow the Illinois-based construction company, Gold Construction, founded by his father, Andreas Stephanopolus. Mark distinguished himself early on in HBS through his defense and promotion of sustainable business practices. His community leadership, however, became most evident in his final term as his activism in this field and canny use of social media resulted in a major investigation into the business practices of Boston-based building titan Stanco Bros. by both the Massachusetts Board of Building Regulations and Standards and the Massachusetts Attorney General's Office, Antitrust Division.

Stephanopolus also founded and popularized the HBS Students for Sustainability, which promises to become a growing force in the shift towards ecologically-sensitive teachings both at Harvard and around the globe.

Obviously not a pushover—Stephanopolus this year also captained the Harvard hockey team, the HBS Blades, as they won back the McCarthur Cup in a rousing victory over the Tuck School of Business team, 6-3—this Dean's Award winner is most known for his quiet-but-determined commitment to holding businesses to a higher standard in both how they choose and how they pursue their goals.

Asked what inspired him most about his time at Harvard, Stephanopolus said, "Honestly, while HBS teaches its students more about the wide theory and process of business than they could find anywhere else, I personally learned more this last year from people outside the school than in. Sometimes a person you spend only a short time with, a week, a few days even, can shape your thinking and your life more than anything else. If they're the right person."

Given that Stephanopolus is apparently known for his openness and became an unofficial crisis counselor for a number of struggling students…

But Ronnie had stopped reading by this point. Her eyes had misted over and her chest had squeezed so tight she found it hard to breathe.

The article was accompanied by a head-and-shoulders picture of each of the Dean's Award winners and the one beside Mark's name looked recent. He stared out of her computer screen at her with something in his eyes she was sure was meant for her.

She'd half-expected him to show up at her graduation ceremony, in fact, for no other reason than she'd gradually developed, over the last few months, a belief that she and Mark were actually destined to be together.

She'd taken steps to make it possible—worked out a deal with Chester and Rolf, finally and definitively ended her relationship with Louis—but hadn't actually talked with *Mark* about any of it. According to her dad and Alex, Mark wasn't seeing anyone else and was completely immersed in a rush of new projects he'd amazingly managed to line up for Gold Construction. Particularly because the Stancos had wisely decided not to sue and Woodwand had broken ground on its new factory just outside Mayville, with Gold Construction signed up as its primary builder.

But Mark not having another girlfriend was no guarantee that he'd be even willing to speak to Ronnie after how she'd not only run out on him, but effectively shut down every attempt he'd made, in the months following her last phone call, to reestablish their lines of communication.

Lines of communication. Ha. See, she'd even learned business-speak for him. Fat lot of—

"Hey, sis!"

It was Alex, the goofball, who'd amazingly had a week off this June between training and his first official posting as a signals intelligence officer, and took a day of it to fly up to Chicago to see her graduate. He'd been out walking the campus with their parents while Ronnie had gone back to her apartment before they all went out to dinner. Now he was poking his head in through her apartment door without knocking.

She looked at her watch. It was time.

Gathering up her things quickly, she joined Alex in the hall outside her apartment.

"So when Mom and Dad head back to Mayville tomorrow…" he began.

"I'm going with them."

"What?"

"Stuff to check out. I've got a few days off."

"Stuff to check out like…" Alex raised his eyebrows.

"Stuff."

As Alex led her down to where he'd parked their parents' Taurus, more comfortable for the ride than the pickup, he shook his head. "Damn, I wish I could be there to see it."

"See what?"

He grinned. "Stuff."

She punched him on the shoulder and they climbed into the car to go find their mom and dad.

21

MARK TOOK A MOMENT to turn his face to the Friday morning sun. The weather had been hot for June, bright and mid-eighties down in Mayville. A degree or two cooler up here on Putter's Ridge with the cool breezes. Felt like God kissing your skin.

It should have made him feel blessed.

Everything was going so well. Where he stood now was about a hundred yards down from the first twelve homes which he'd shown to the Clearys back in December in their unfinished state. Those houses were now all fully finished, sold, and one-third occupied. And down where Mark stood, the smell in the air was of fresh-turned dirt, diesel fuel, and men's sweat because they'd broken ground on most of the new section of upscale homes that promised to be even more beautiful than the first.

With the Woodwand contract firmly in place and moving ahead off the south end of Mayville itself, *plus* two subcontracting jobs underway in neighboring towns, Gold Construction was rolling in cash. True, its full-time personnel were getting stretched, but Mark had been reviewing resumes and talking to all his contacts about people to fill management positions for weeks. This was a natural part of boom times and one to savor, not complain about.

He had the Harvard MBA. He had the respect of his peers not just here in the Midwest but, because of the incredible clash he'd had with the Stancos, nationwide. He had no question that if he ever decided to leave Gold Construction, he could either join an international building group, or jump fields entirely. Get headhunted to some exciting startup doing anything from microchips to chains of sushi restaurants.

He was achieving. He was successful. He was admired.

He was empty.

He was also angry, he realized. Because, despite all the good things they'd said about him at his Harvard Business School commencement, he felt like he was become nothing more than a sly, driven businessman. Yes, he'd fought for justice. And won. And saved his father's company.

But the person who'd really inspired him to do it, no matter how he looked at it, had rejected him. He'd offered her everything and she'd left him for another man. He'd even virtually come crawling on his knees after her when she left, calling her not once or twice but...what? Four times? Five? Six? Enough times that, despite Professor Krizansky's pithy advice about having patience and trust, he'd finally concluded he was a stupid shmuck who should just accept that, as it had been so hip to say a few years back, she just wasn't "into" him.

Especially after he learned that she'd broken up with Louis and *still* hadn't called him. That had stuck deep in a throat of pride he hadn't fully realized he had.

So he'd stopped planning for her. Tried to stop caring.

It was done.

He truly hoped Ronnie was happy. He couldn't believe she was. Not after standing up for him with Carl Hemsler, then calling Mark to tell him what she'd done and that she was listening to her heart. And not *even letting him speak with her for three months?*

But it was done.

"Marcario!"

Mark turned to see his father climbing out of his car at the south end of the first stage development cul-de-sac. Andreas Stephanopolus stepped over the curb and came walking gingerly down the steep-and-unfinished weedy slope towards Mark's chewed-up earth.

Mark hurried up the slope to meet him, got to him halfway down and then walked down the rest of the way beside him, just in case.

"Pop, what are you—?"

His father waved him silent. "We have to drive back into town now. For a meeting at the mall you are redeveloping."

"*Maybe* redeveloping."

This would be the Bark Street Mall, where he'd had one of his first un-chaperoned conversations with Ronnie last Christmas. Since then the Wool Barn owner had decided to retire and didn't want to sell her business, just shut it down. Because it was on the end of the strip, the mall owner had wanted to tear it down completely to add to the parking space. Mark, still in his hopeful phase, had talked him into holding it for just awhile to see if anyone might want to take it over and start up a new small business there.

"Yes. Yes. That's the point, Marcario. Someone interested in the space. Come."

He gave a bitter smile. Great. Another possible job. He should be happy, right? He just felt annoyed. "You know who?"

His father shrugged in a weird way. "New store."

Mark sighed. Something strange then. But Mark pointed his father to the second-hand pickup truck he'd bought off Stony Phelps when all the Harvard celebrations were done. "Okay, Pop," he said. "We'll come back for your truck later. Let's go meet them, shall we?"

22

IT WAS ONE OF LIFE'S CRUELEST JOKES, Ronnie thought as she stood in the hot sun in front of the closed Wool Barn store in the Bark Street Mall, that, at life's most important moments, you always had to pee.

She glanced at her smartphone, estimating the time it would have taken for Andreas Stephanopolus to have hung up the phone from her, then driven up to the Putter's Ridge project where he'd said Mark was working and talked him into coming down. Add in Mark's time driving down and—

It didn't matter! She wasn't going to meet Mark in this state.

She hurried north along the front sidewalk to the Dover Pantry, where she'd greeted Beppe Mammazza earlier, and asked to use his bathroom. She emerged five minutes later, feeling refreshed and much better, to see a pickup truck swing into an empty parking space in front of the Wool Barn.

And just the briefest flash of strong shoulders and dark curly hair moving in the driver's seat—putting the truck in park and off, unclipping the seatbelt—were enough to start

Ronnie's heart racing. She tried to swallow with her suddenly-dry mouth, rubbed her hands down the front of the light cotton dress she'd worn for this meeting. It was a Dolce & Gabbana imitation in white-and-green jewel tones that cinched in around the waist and complemented her figure without being too obvious. She wore her hair shorter now than Mark would remember, but it was freshly washed and styled and hadn't started to frizz from the heat yet. She'd kept the makeup minimal, almost nonexistent, to match at least that much of how she'd been last Christmas.

She was as pretty and fresh, in other words, as she knew how to make herself. Her father had stared at her, dumbstruck, when she'd come down after breakfast and asked to borrow the Taurus. Her mother had nodded approvingly.

And Ronnie herself just felt…terrified.

But now Mark and his father were out of the truck and standing in front of the boarded-up Wool Barn, looking around. Mark looked seriously peeved.

Fighting hard to breathe through the pounding of her heart, Ronnie walked along the storefront walkway towards them.

~~~~

When Mark and his father stepped onto the cracked-concrete walkway in front of the closed Wool Barn, there was no one there. Perfect. It was either a bad joke, then, or whoever it was that had said they'd meet them here was so disrespectful or sloppy that they'd wandered off somewhere or just not bothered to arrive yet.

It didn't bode well for any future dealings with them.

Then it was like there was a sea change in the air. Like something in his peripheral senses made everything fresher and brighter.

He swiveled his head and saw her. For a second, he wondered if he'd been working too hard, pushing such long hours that he was now into fatigue-induced mirages. Because she *looked* like a mirage—curvy and cool in rich blues and greens and reds, her hair shorter but the same flaming red he remembered, her face even more open, the lips barely parted, the emerald eyes seeking his.

Then he slammed back to earth and felt the underarm sweat staining his work shirt, the dirt all over his jeans. Not to mention the permanent squint and scowl he seemed unable to tear off his face most days.

He also felt his heart swell up with a load of hurt and resentment that fought to shove out the automatic eagerness that filled his limbs and quickened his breath.

"Hello, Mark," she said and he heard the quaver in her voice.

Good! There *should* be a quaver there! What did she think? That she could just waltz back into town like this on a visit to her parents, see him, and expect him to sit up and beg like some pathetic hound dog she could flip the occasional treat to in between kicking him to the curb?

"Hi." About as cold as he knew how to make it. He saw that register on her face and it made the twist in his gut even worse.

She touched her hair with a shaky hand. He'd so loved it long. It had always been a surprise, full of life, whenever he'd seen it. This length, it looked so…controlled. Stylish. Beautiful even, heartbreakingly so. But…controlled.

"You cut your hair," he said stupidly.

"Recently. Yes." She bit her upper lip. "I'm…trying to get my head around being a businesswoman."

"I thought you were a candy maker."

"I am. I can be both. I finished my degree, you know."

"I heard. Why?"

"You mean why am I telling you? Or why…?"

Mark wanted to turn his head to one side, look away to show how little he truly cared. But the fact was he couldn't take his eyes off her face. Every little curve of it. Every little twitch. "Why did you finish your degree? I thought you'd chucked all that traditional stuff and were doing what you wanted."

"Yes, but—"

"Even chucked Louis. Good for you on that, by the way. Have you started seeing someone new?"

"I…I haven't had much time…"

"Of course you haven't."

~~~~

Ronnie's insides were shaking to pieces. The *anger* in his voice. The *bitterness*. Oh, goodness, she'd waited too long.

She'd wanted to prove herself to herself. To him. To find the courage to be able to offer something real to him versus more painful waffling and angst. But she'd waited too long and the connection they'd had was burned completely away into ash and charcoal.

"I...I've been putting together a business plan," she managed, wanting to look away, maybe greet Mark's father, who was standing behind his right shoulder, maybe pretend to casually check out all the other shoppers milling around the Bark Street Mall on this beautiful June day that smelled of pine trees and lilac bushes.

But she couldn't tear her gaze from his. Like he de*manded* her attention. Like she *owed* it to him.

"A business plan for what?" he asked her now. "You're finally opening up your own shop in Chicago to compete with Chester's?"

She gasped a little and found herself feeling braced by the warm June air. "I don't want to compete with Chester's. I'm in partnership with them. Opening a second shop with that name, but that I'm running. We plan to share recipes."

He frowned at her, his square face so dark in expression it seemed to suck all the sun she'd just bolstered herself with, right out of her. "Where are you opening it?"

She blinked. "I thought you knew. Right here. Where the Wool Barn used to be."

~~~~

Ronnie had just said something, but Mark couldn't figure out what it was. Where the Wool Barn used to be? But that was here. In this mall. In Mayville. Was there another Wool Barn in Chicago?

But she'd said *Right here.*

"Here?" he said.

She bobbed her head a little, giving him a scared smile. "I…sort of thought that maybe you'd fought to keep this space available in case I wanted it. My dad thought that."

No. This wasn't right. Something was just not right here. "You're…planning to open up a Chester's in rinky-dink little Mayville."

"That's right. Only, my dad's been sending me projections of the town's growth and Mayville's not going to be so rinky-dink in a year or two. Still small-town character, he hopes, but the numbers are here now to support a shop like Chester's. If it's run well. If I do it right."

Okay, that was a *little* better. At least she wasn't simpering any longer. He didn't know a Ronnie Cleary who simpered. And a simperer couldn't run a successful business.

"You've got a plan, do you?" he said.

"I've got a plan, a website, and an online ordering and shipping program I'm co-developing with Chester and Rolf to supply the entire Midwest."

"Hunh. And the coasts?"

"We'll ship there if they order. But the plan is to open a third and fourth Chester's by year five. Spread the joy."

Now she was bubbling. Now her eyes were sparking like her hair. He could feel that energy push its way into his heart and shove out the great black cloud of resentment and hurt he'd been carrying there. There was no room for it when the desire and longing and his soul-deep *need* for her kept growing so quickly.

"Ambitious," he said.

"No more than taking on one of the biggest building companies in the country and getting them charged with all sorts of statutory breaches."

He bowed his head slightly, feeling a tiny spark of hope at the way she'd said it. Admiration. Approval. Forgiveness?

"Okay," he said. "So let me ask you something. Why here in Mayville? You could have gone straight to the coasts. Or further south. Was it just because your mom and dad live here? Because I seem to recall you saying you loved them to pieces but could never live with them anymore."

She gave him a look of utter incredulity, her eyebrows high, chin hanging. "You're asking if I'm looking to set up in Mayville just to be closer to my folks? Seriously?"

"Seriously."

He held his breath, waiting for her answer.

~~~~

It was there. Was it there? Ronnie swore she'd seen it flicker in there beneath the tough, angry mask Mark had worn since he'd seen her. He still cared for her. Cared but was hurt. Cared but was as scared as she was.

For all his battling giants. For all his early cocksure wooing of her when they first met as adults this last Christmas. Yes, he'd wrestle for the things he truly wanted. He'd fight tooth and nail for them.

But now, because of all that had happened and how. And because, ultimately, you couldn't *win* someone to you; you could only *invite* them; they had to make the decision to join you on your path.

Because of all that, it was her turn.

"So are you going to tell the boy?" said a voice behind her. Beppe Mammazza, who, like a good thirty or more people from around the mall, Ronnie now realized, had gathered around this little standoff she and Mark were having. Like they'd become a circus event or something. Some of the faces she recognized. Some of them probably even knew the story of what was going on here. More, she was sure, had just been drawn because there was obviously something going on.

She turned her face back to Beppe and held a finger to her lips. Then turned back to Mark. This ultimately wasn't for Beppe, or Mark's father who also seemed to be holding his breath behind Mark's right shoulder, or any of the other people gathered around. This was just her and Mark. Here and now.

"Mark," she said slowly. "Marcario Stephanopolus. You suggested to me almost six months ago that it would be possible for us to be together if I didn't have to be tied to Chicago."

"*I* was ready to move to Chicago," he broke in, face intense. "Did you know that?"

She held her finger up to his lips to shush him like she'd shushed Beppe. "And I couldn't see you doing that at the time. I was too tangled up with commitments and doubts and questions."

She held up her finger again as he looked ready to interrupt, and he settled back on his feet, listening hard.

"It has taken me almost six months to untangle all those strings so my heart could see what should have been crystal clear to it all along."

She tilted her head to look at him listening to her. He was such a force of nature, strong and handsome and good, and so much more doggedly determined than she could have imagined was possible.

"And what it's seen is really simple. I love you. I want to make a life with you if you'll have me. And I'll make that life with you wherever you are, wherever you live. Here in Mayville. Off in New York. Wherever. But since you're here in Mayville for now, to help out your dad with his company that may be your company one day, yes?"

Mark's father nodded vigorously from behind Mark's shoulder.

"Then I figured I better find a way to do what I'm passionate about here in Mayville. Close to my mother and father, yes. But more importantly, critically, close to you."

She blushed. "And incidentally, I'm sorry for the way I ran out on you just before New Year's. It was stupid. Based on what I thought were pretty reasonable assumptions but…stupid. I beg your apology, your love, and your help in converting this old Wool Barn shop into the second Chester's, my first official Ronnie-Cleary-run sweets shop, in the country."

She stopped and waited. Mark was silent, just staring hard at her.

"Um…yes?" she said.

There was another long pause, then Mark nodded slowly. "Yes," he said. "To all of it. My forgiveness. My help, of course. And, through all my anger and pain and struggle, my love. For you. Probably the strongest single thing that's kept me going."

"Um…"

"Psst," whispered Beppe, behind her. "Step into his arms and kiss him now."

So she did.

And when they were done, and she returned from the buzzing, heart-pounding, minty-tasting wonder of it to hear the cheering applause of their audience, she pulled back and saw something she had so missed for so many months—Mark grinning broadly at her.

"You taste like cinnamon," he said. "I love cinnamon."

"Smooth talker. You have the keys to the place that's going to become my version of Chester's Sweets?"

His fished in his jeans pocket and came up with the key. "Another kiss first."

She happily paid the fee, took the key, and they entered the future together.

ABOUT THE AUTHOR

Terri Darling lives with her family in the Pacific Northwest, where she writes sensual, suspenseful, and sweet romance. You can find more about her and her work at www.terridarling.com.

Did you know...

Most of Terri Darling's sweet romance so far has been short fiction that's available individually (in e-book form) and in collections of five or ten stories that will have you believing in love again!

Five sweet romance tales of how love sneaks in when we least expect it. Feel the vulnerability of a woman who wins the lead in a community theater play opposite a cad she's always wanted in "Love in the Wings." Breathe the ocean air and possibilities in "Footprints in the Sand." And more.

You can find these...

and other novels by Terri Darling at your favorite online bookstore or through www.terridarling.com.

Five sweet romance stories of love stepping up to make life that much better. Follow a woman who will never again let anyone tell her she can't do something. Risk embarrassment in a swimsuit shop. Laugh as an online relationship gets real. And more. Contains "Upwards," "The Swimsuit Shop," "Persistence Pays," "The True Face of Love," and "The Second Time Around."

www.ingramcontent.com/pod-product-compliance
Lightning Source LLC
Chambersburg PA
CBHW030959260626
47169CB00002B/609